MAGIC & MOCHAS

TALES OF LOVE & LORE

VANNA WOODS

Magic & Mochas

Copyright © 2025 by Vanna Woods

All rights reserved.

No part of this publication may be reproduced, distributed, or transmitted in any form or by any means, including photocopying, recording, or other electronic or mechanical methods, without the prior written permission of the publisher, except as permitted by U.S. copyright law. For permission requests, contact the author at vannawoodsbooks@gmail.com.

The story, all names, characters, and incidents portrayed in this production are fictitious. No identification with actual persons (living or deceased), places, buildings, and products is intended or should be inferred.

Book Cover by Estheticah Cover Designs

Ebook ISBN: 978-1-965196-10-6

Paperback ISBN: 978-1-965196-11-3

Hardcover ISBN: 978-1-965196-12-0

Enjoy the magic
in every cozy day
Vanna Woods

For anyone who has ever found comfort in a warm drink, a purring cat, or a story that feels like home.

CHAPTER ONE

Home & Heartbreak

CLOVE

Three days after hexing my ex's underwear drawer, I came home to Willowmere with nothing but my grimoire, my cat, and a very expensive espresso machine.

My parents' little cottage looked exactly as I remembered it: peeling purple paint with black window shutters and a shingle roof, with ivy climbing up the sides and marigolds and snapdragons cascading from the window boxes. Despite the fact that it was October, all of the plants were magically enchanted to bloom year-round. Smoke puffed in a wide array of colors from the chimney—most likely from my mother's latest potion brew. And the organized chaos of the front garden was neatly guarded by a wrought-iron fence, upon which a raven perched.

The purple cottage fit in perfectly with the other craftsman-style houses that lined the street. But what made the quaint town of Willowmere so special was not the architecture of the houses or even the main street, which was filled with mom and pop shops, but the residents themselves.

Willowmere was one of the only magical communities in the state of Washington where all kinds of extraordinary creatures could live together in harmony. Normally, witches, werewolves, faeries and orcs dwelled only with their own kind. But in Willowmere, you could find just about every sort of magical folk you could imagine.

Humans were the one exception; there was a ward around town that prevented humans from accidentally stumbling in. It was a marvel of magical engineering—a fact which my father would never let me forget. It *was* our family's proudest achievement, after all.

And now that I was moving back in at the ripe old age of twenty-seven, I was certain I would get to hear all about it. *Again.*

With a sigh, I lugged my heavy suitcase along behind me as I approached the front gate. I waved a hand to unlock it, and the raven croaked at me in greeting. My mother's familiar, Fig, cocked his head at me, then flew inside through an open window—no doubt, to announce my arrival.

Are you sure I can't eat it? My own familiar, Silas, asked me telepathically. The black cat twined around my ankles, but his eyes were riveted on the window. *Not even a little nibble?*

You know better than that, I chided him. *Familiars eating other familiars is strictly forbidden.*

Never liked that law, he grumbled. He trotted up to the front door, which he magically opened and shut behind himself—right in my face.

"Bratty cat," I mumbled.

I heard that!

You were supposed to! Though I could hardly blame him. I wasn't exactly thrilled with our new living arrangements, either.

When I approached the front door, it swung open, as if the house itself were welcoming me home. The smell of apple cider teased my nose as I stepped inside, and I smiled, despite myself.

No matter how long it had been, this place would always feel like home.

My mother swept into the entryway from the kitchen, with her raven perched on her shoulder. "Clove Morelli! Fig just told me you arrived. I wasn't expecting you till this evening!"

I let her pull me into one of her motherly hugs. "I took a flying carriage to avoid the traffic."

"Oh, let me look at you. It's been far too long since your last visit." Ginger Morelli held me at arms' length, her blue eyes scanning me from head to toe. She was dressed in the black-lace style that most witches favored, and kept her dark hair drawn up in a bun.

"Welcome home, pumpkin," my dad said as he came around the corner. Tristan Morelli stood a head taller than my mother, though it was his green eyes and dark purple hair that always made him stand out in a crowd. His bit of a belly told me mom must have been baking more frequently since I'd left home.

I'd always thought that I was a perfect combination of the two, with my turquoise eyes and black hair with purple undertones. I liked to think my own style of dress was a tad more...modern, however. I preferred leather boots over ones with pointed, curly toes, and purple dresses over black-on-black, lacey colonial outfits.

"Thanks, dad." I mustered a half-smile for him.

"Why don't you go upstairs and unpack? Dinner will be ready in just a few minutes." Mom patted me on the shoulder, but I noticed how her eyes kept darting away from my left ring-finger, like butterflies afraid to land.

I nodded. "I'll only be a minute."

Wandering down the hall and up the stairs, I glanced at all of the family portraits that my mother had hung with such pride. Accomplished witches and warlocks, every last one of them.

Continuing on down the hall, I entered the last door on the left. My childhood bedroom looked exactly as I remembered it: Spellbooks and romance novels lined my bookshelves, and a worn woolen rug blanketed the hardwood floor. Warm rays from the setting sun filtered in through my white curtains and dappled the small desk in the corner. Silas was already curled up on top of my bed's lavender duvet cover, snoring away.

Quietly, I unzipped my suitcase and carefully lifted my espresso machine onto my desk. After a quick examination to make sure it hadn't been scratched, I threw the handful of tops and pants I had used to swaddle it into my tiny closet. Finally, I placed my grimoire on top of my dresser.

I had been *so* upset, that I had left everything else behind. But going back for the rest of my things was out of the question.

Without waking Silas, I slipped out and headed for the dining room. Mom finished setting the table as I walked in.

"You're just in time. I was about to ladle some chili into your bread bowl. I made the sourdough fresh this morning," she said with a wink.

My mouth watered. Mom's sourdough was my favorite. No matter how many times I tried to make it, mine just never came out quite right.

She served the food, and the three of us sat down around the table to eat. The blend of spices in the apple cider was divine, and her chili warmed me from the inside out, though the warmth stopped just shy of my heart.

The sounds of splashing spoons and glasses clinking filled the air, but after a while, my mother asked tentatively, "Do you want to talk about it?"

A lump rose in my throat. "Not yet."

She nodded one too many times. A hint of tension laced the air, until my dad cleared his throat and prompted, "Ginger, why don't you tell Clove all about Mrs. Virgil's news?"

I perked up. "Mrs. Virgil?"

The satyr had run a cute little café on main street for as long as I could remember. I loved spending time there after school when I was little, sipping iced coffees while I did my spellwork.

My mom eagerly latched onto the topic. "Yes, that's right! After her last child went off to college, she decided to travel the world, and left early last year. She's been planning this trip for ages; I know there are at least seven different forests and five branches of the family she wanted to visit."

"That's wonderful news!" She had always worked so hard on her café, so I was happy to hear she was taking a little vacation for herself. "Which one of her children took over the family business?"

Mom and dad exchanged a look. It was a look I knew all too well, the one that meant they had bad news they didn't want to break to me.

"Pumpkin, the thing is...none of her children had any interest in running the café. Mrs. Virgil shut it down and put the building up for sale." He smiled sadly. "Though it hasn't sold yet."

My spoon froze halfway to my mouth. "What?!" How could *none* of her kids have wanted to continue the thriving family business? There were *seven* of them, for crying out loud!

Had they *all* decided to be adventurers or apothecaries or something? "The café is...gone?"

"I'm afraid so." My mom patted my hand comfortingly. "I know how much you loved spending time there. It's a shame to think of it sitting empty—both the café and the apartment above it."

I slowly lowered my spoon as a crazy, completely ridiculous idea popped into my head. "How much..." I licked my lips. "How much is she asking for it? For the building, I mean?"

The dreams of a younger me flitted through my mind. Dreams of running my own cozy little café, one filled with the aroma of coffee and the sound of music and laughter. And as impossible as it once seemed, perhaps the only thing holding me back now was myself.

For once in my life, I was done putting someone else's dreams before my own.

Plus, since it came with an apartment, I could move out of my parents' house and get a shred of my independence and dignity back.

My parents exchanged another look. Mom pulled out her magically expanding bag and rifled through it, until she pulled out a flyer and handed it to me. "This is the asking price. But why do you want to know?"

I scanned the flyer, my turquoise eyes quickly finding the number I was looking for. If I drained my savings, I should be able to afford the down payment. Barely. "Because I'm going to buy it."

"Now, pumpkin, take some time to think this through. I know you used to love that old café, but you don't need to give up on your bright future in the big city to save it." Concern creased my dad's forehead.

"I *have* thought about it. For longer than you might guess." My heart was racing, but my voice was steady. I had promised myself that one day, if the opportunity presented itself to escape the rat race, I would take it.

Everyday in my corporate job, I had dreamed of living a slower life, a cozier life. One where I answered to no one except myself, and where I could sip my morning coffee while looking out at my little garden or flower boxes before opening my shop for the day. One where I could finally wear all the cute little dresses and frocks shoved in the back of my closet, and come home before the sun set. A life that truly felt like mine—a life worth living.

Even if that looked different from what I was *supposed* to want. From what my *parents* wanted for me. From what everyone else *expected* of me.

My mom took my hands, the calluses on her palms from a lifetime of working as a hedgewitch feeling like sandpaper against my skin. "Sweetie, we just want what's best for you. We want you to be able to do all of the things we never could."

"I know." Guilt wormed its way through my heart. My parents had never had the opportunity to go to college, or to leave Willowmere. My mom had worked her fingers to the bone to give me that chance.

Was I a terrible daughter for throwing it away?

My dad put a hand on his wife's shoulder, his green eyes softening. "Owning a small business is no picnic. Are you certain this is what will make you happy?"

"I am." I would take mopping floors and polishing glasses over drafting spreadsheets and office politics any day. And at least here, I would not have to hide my magic like I did in the city of Seattle.

"Then I will arrange a meeting with the real estate agent for you in the morning."

"Tristan!" My mom protested, but he simply patted her shoulder.

"We will support your decision, as long as it makes you happy. Besides, it will be nice to see you more often—especially during the holidays." His words seemed to ease mom's worries.

"Always ganging up on me, you two," she tutted. "But it *would* be lovely to see you more often, sweetie."

"Thank you." I smiled, and for the first time in quite a while, it wasn't fake.

The next morning, I knocked on the real estate agent's door the very moment he flipped the CLOSED sign to OPEN. Though the centaur who answered the door looked none too happy about it.

"Good morning, Mr. Chevalier! I believe my father sent a raven to say I'd be stopping by to purchase the old café on main street this morning." I'd been too excited to sleep, so I had stayed up most of the night imagining how to renovate the space and what to call my new business. After much deliberation, I had settled on a name I liked: The Broom & Bean.

"Is that what the letter says?" He tried, unsuccessfully, to cover a yawn, while glancing at a table behind him.

Beyond his bay horse's hindquarters, I was just able to make out the letter sitting unopened on the table. He glared at me from behind his half-moon spectacles, and scratched at his long beard.

This was not going well. But fortunately, I had come prepared!

"Coffee?" I held out to him the second cup I had brewed like an offering.

"Thanks." When he took a sip, his eyes lit up. "Hey, that's not bad. Please, come in."

He sidestepped so I could enter, before closing the door behind me. His receiving room was spacious and tasteful, with an oval table at standing height and a few stools on one side for two-legged guests. Scenic photos of houses and buildings he had sold lined the beige walls, and decorative plants stood in the corners.

I noticed with some amusement a bite had been taken out of a few of the leaves.

Mr. Chevalier clip-clopped over to the table, the sound of his horseshoes rapping sharply on the hardwood floors. It suddenly occurred to me why centaurs never even tried to sneak up on people—it was evidently an effort in futility.

"So, you are interested in purchasing Mrs. Virgil's old café building?" he clarified as I took a seat on one of the stools. He slid the same flyer over to me that my parents had.

"Precisely. I have the twenty percent down payment check ready, and I brought all of my relevant paperwork, including my credit score report and my financial statements." I handed him the folder I had prepared after he took another long sip of his coffee.

After flipping through the documents for a few minutes, he nodded. "Everything seems to be in order. I can have my contact at the bank set up the mortgage with an interest rate slightly lower than the human market's."

"That would be much appreciated." I had done the calculations around dawn, and so long as I earned a certain amount from the business each month, I should be able to make the monthly mortgage payments without too much trouble. "I would like to move in and open my coffee shop as soon as possible."

"A coffee shop, eh? You'll give the diner a run for its money—at least when it comes to the morning coffee rush." He glanced up at me quickly, before looking down again and shuffling through a packet of documents with text so tiny it made my eyes hurt to try and read them. "I'll just need you to sign here, here, and here, and check the box stating you wish to purchase the building as-is, sight unseen."

"Sight unseen?" I asked, a bit nervously. "What does that mean?"

"Oh, it's just legal jargon for buying the property without first inspecting it." He waved a hand in the air, as if batting away my concerns. "Since you already know how you want to use the space, it's not as if you need to figure out where to put the counter and the register. All of that is still in place from the previous business."

"Right." I nodded slowly. "I guess that makes sense."

Why did I get the feeling there was a question I didn't know I needed to ask? Or that I was missing something? The agent seemed like he was in a hurry to get me to sign on the dotted line.

But I *had* already decided that nothing could stop me. Even if there were an infestation of pixies in the upstairs apartment that he thought would be a problem, I would deal with it.

I signed my name with a flourish, thrilled beyond words to finally be taking the first step in the direction of my dreams. The contract rolled itself up, and with a flash and a popping sound, teleported itself to the bank.

"Here is the key to the shop, the mailbox, and...the upstairs apartment." Mr. Chevalier handed me three keys, the metal cold and solid against my skin.

"Thank you so much! I am going to get to work right away. Enjoy your coffee—once I open, I'll charge you the friends and family rate," I said as I stood and headed for the door.

But as I closed it with a wave of my hand, I could have sworn I heard him mutter, "Good luck."

CHAPTER TWO

Lounging & Loneliness

THORNE

With a silent command, I summoned a soldier made of living shadow, and ordered it to clean up the kitchen now that I'd finished my breakfast. My violet eyes watched its empty, glowing ones as it systematically swept the floor and wiped down the countertops.

This ability was what made me practically a one-man army when it came to raids and conquering dungeons. But it was also the reason not a single old bag in this entire little town would rent to me.

My reputation had preceded me.

Hence why I was now squatting in this empty apartment above a closed café. Although I had been hanging around town for the better part of a year, none of the residents had been brave enough to chase me out yet. Sure, the dirty looks stung, but I was used to that. And so long as I didn't threaten them or draw too much attention to myself, the townsfolk had no reason to take up arms against me.

Not that they would win.

Well, maybe if the fire drakes, witches, and vampires coordinated their attacks, they might pose a bit of a challenge. But this was a sleepy town, and I was certain I had more combat experience than all of them combined.

After all, what else was a shadowmancer like me meant to do for work?

Gruesome flashbacks played behind my eyes: the loss of friends, the endless hordes of monsters, and the scent of blood and betrayal.

I rose abruptly from the kitchen table and stalked to the room I had claimed as my own. Nothing good ever came of sitting still, and yet there wasn't much else for me to do. At least cooking could take my mind off of things three times a day.

Having completed its tasks, my shadow soldier followed me on silent feet.

Your next orders, Lord Thorne? Its voice spoke directly into my mind in a raspy whisper.

Rest until I summon you next.

As you wish. With a respectful bow, it melted into a pool of wispy shadows, which crept into my own shadow. Though my soldiers were efficient at executing orders, none of them had much in the way of personality. Or original thought.

It was next to impossible to hold even a bland conversation about the weather with them.

So even though I always had an army with me, I was perennially alone.

Back when I had been in the thick of an endless stream of battles, I had dreamed of a solitary future like this. But now that I had it...

It felt empty.

Angrily, I pulled open my dresser drawer and piled some clean clothes on the bed. There was no use getting down in the dumps about things I couldn't control. Even if I could manipulate other people's reactions to me, I would always know their acceptance wasn't real.

And that would only make me feel worse.

Maybe it would be better if I tried to blend into the human world, instead. Perhaps if I joined their military, I could fit in *there.* But would I be able to resist the urge to use my powers to save a brother-in-arm's life if it came down to it?

I was fairly certain the answer was a resounding *no.*

And then I would be on the run in both the human *and* magical worlds.

But what else was I supposed to do, sit around moping for the rest of my life? That didn't sound particularly appealing, either.

With a heavy sigh, I collected my bundle of clothes and headed to the bathroom. A cold shower always helped me clear my thoughts.

CHAPTER THREE

Surprises & Strangers

CLOVE

Willowmere's main street unfurled like a ribbon of old cobblestone, gently winding through the heart of the town like it had grown there on purpose, rather than being built.

Each storefront shimmered with enchantments—wooden signs that spelled their names in curling script one moment and blossomed into floral carvings the next. The bakery's windows glowed with soft pinks and oranges, and the bookshop's awning ruffled itself like feathers when stirred by the soft breeze. Pumpkins carved with softly flickering faces lined the stoops, and ivy crept up every stone wall in shifting hues of green, copper, and plum.

As I strolled slowly along the sidewalk, the morning sun warmed my skin like an old friend's embrace. Spiced cider, old parchment, roasted hazelnut, and the welcome aroma of baking bread hung in the crisp autumn air. The diner's cinnamon-scented steam curled lazily into the sky, mingling with the honeyed smoke from a nearby candlemaker. Even the cobblestones themselves seemed to exhale the scent of old magic—earthy, warm, and faintly electric, like the air before a storm.

Windchimes tinkled peacefully when I came to a stop in front of the building that was now mine. Mrs. Virgil's old sign still hung above the door, but the windows were all boarded up and cobwebs hung from the eaves. The brick facade was looking rather faded, though the ivy around the corners seemed to be doing just fine. The awnings, on the other hand, were a tattered mess.

If this was why the centaur had seemed nervous, he needn't have worried. Minor cleaning and repairs were no obstacle for a witch.

With a wave of my hand and some purple sparks, I repaired the awnings, changing the pink stripes to purple, and burned away the boards and cobwebs. The swinging sign magically cleaned itself, and the script writing changed to read: The Broom & Bean.

With a grin nearly too big for my face, I unlocked the beautiful French door. The glass of the window was cracked, but I would enjoy coming up with a stained glass scene to replace it. As I stepped inside, I sent warm balls of witchlight to hover by the rafters.

The inside of the café looked a little like I felt: empty. But with some time and a lot of work, we could both be bright and hopeful again.

Golden morning light filtered through the dirty windowpanes, casting soft, smudged rectangles across the scuffed wooden floor. The floorboards creaked with each step, as though waking reluctantly from a long sleep. Cobwebs draped like lace from the corners of the ceiling, and a crooked ceiling fan hung frozen in mid-turn. The counters were covered with a thick layer of dust, and the pastry case I had once fogged with my breath now stood dark and empty.

The tables sat askew, mismatched chairs tucked in or scattered like guests who'd left mid-conversation. A once-charming fireplace at the far end of the space was choked with ash and old parchments, one of which floated gently to the floor when I entered, as if sighing in relief at my return.

In the corner, an ancient bulletin board still held flyers for past events: *Herb Swap Night, Full Moon Readings,* and *Tarot & Toast Tuesdays.* The edges had curled, but the magic ink shimmered faintly when I looked too long.

It was a good thing Silas had opted to stay curled up on my bed this morning—he would have had a sneezing fit, and I never would have heard the end of it.

Overall, it wasn't terrible. Hopefully, I could get it up and running before the Moonlit Masquerade Ball at the end of the month, on Halloween.

The first thing I did was open the windows to let in some fresh air. But before getting to work, I decided to head upstairs to take a look at the apartment. If it wasn't completely unliveable, I might even be able to move in tonight!

Entering the back storage area, I moved through the space like a wraith. I found the stairway that led up to the second level, and unlocked the apartment's door with the key the centaur had given me.

But when I stepped inside, I frowned. Unlike the café downstairs, the apartment didn't look abandoned at all. The curtains were drawn over the windows, and the living room was cozy and inviting, with thick carpeting and a plush sofa. I ran a finger along the fireplace mantel, but no dust came off. The kitchen was practically spotless, and even had a bowl of fresh fruit on the dining table.

Had Mrs. Virgil purchased a preservation spell for the apartment? But if that were the case, then why would she not have used one on the café as well?

Moving down the short hallway, I peeked into the main bedroom. A large four-poster bed took up the center of the room, with a desk and some dressers in the corners. The room felt lived-in, and had a decidedly masculine feel. Had one of her sons lived here right up until Mrs. Virgil left?

And then I heard the toilet flush.

I froze, my heart jumping into my throat. I wasn't alone! Was there really an infestation of pixies here, after all? If that were the case, I needed to kick them out right this second! There was no telling how much damage they might have already done to the walls!

I ran into the hall and made a beeline for the bathroom I had passed earlier. The door was ajar, so I slammed it open, a pixie banishment spell ready at my fingertips.

But instead of pixies, I found myself staring at a very handsome and very *naked* man. He was tall, with a shock of dark hair and the shadow of a goatee on his strong jaw. Scars criss-crossed his chest, and his chiseled abs could have functioned adequately as a washboard. Color rose in my cheeks as I realized he was wearing nothing but his boxers.

The spell fizzled out and died.

"Didn't anyone teach you how to knock?" His voice brushed like velvet against my ears.

My gaze snapped up to his vivid violet eyes, which were watching me with a sort of cold, detached amusement. Keeping my eyes fixed firmly on his marble-worthy face, I blurted, "Who are you and what are you doing in my apartment?"

"*Your* apartment?" Shadows curled up from the floor and wrapped around his shoulders like a cloak made of midnight. "I take it that four-legged grass-snatcher finally managed to sell the building, then?"

"That's right. And since he failed to mention a tenant, I have to assume you are squatting here." Was *this* what Mr. Chevalier had been nervous about? Not an infestation of pixies, but of one grumpy man? "As the new owner, I will need you to vacate. Immediately."

The man glanced slowly down at his state of undress, before cocking one eyebrow at me. "I think not. I will be taking my shower, which you so rudely interrupted. Now, if you'll excuse me."

The shadows came alive once again—in order to slam the door shut in my face. I heard the distinct click of the lock engaging, followed by the sound of running water.

For a moment, I gaped at the door. Then I shut my mouth with a snap and stormed out of the apartment. I was going to need to have a talk with Mr. Chevalier, since he purposely failed to mention one *crucial* little detail.

There was a shadowmancer squatting in my apartment!

I stomped down the stairs, trying not to let my irritation at this unplanned hiccup ruin what little momentum I had managed to scrape together over the last twenty-four hours. The dim and dusty interior of the old café seemed to mock me and my admittedly whimsical aspirations.

Tears pricked at the back of my eyes, but I refused to let them fall. I had promised myself I was done feeling sorry for myself. I would *not* wallow in the all-too-familiar sense of betrayal Mr. Chevalier had just evoked in me. So what if my first interaction with someone outside of my family had turned out to be another sort of betrayal?

It could have been worse—there could have been a werewolf with rabies behind that door instead of a very grumpy and very muscular shadowmancer! My former fiancé didn't hold a candle to *him*.

I sighed. *Focus, Clove.* Moping about wouldn't help me show that bastard of a warlock that I was doing just fine without him. That my heart hadn't been absolutely shattered into a thousand pieces that night.

If heartbreak had a smell, I was convinced it would be burnt caramel and rotten fish with a shot of betrayal—but I was determined to smother it with cinnamon and freshly brewed coffee.

I needed to focus on tackling one problem at a time, and I knew the perfect place to start. After all, the shop wasn't about to clean itself.

So I tied my long, dark hair into a ponytail, hung my coat on a peg, and rolled up my sleeves. After raiding the supply closet, I enchanted all of the items I found there. I sent the duster up to the ceiling to take care of the cobwebs, had a cloth and a bucket of water get to work polishing the windows, and ordered the broom to sweep the floor.

Next, I set about getting the pastry case cleaned out and the counters polished. As I moved behind the counter, I could tell where Mrs. Virgil had kept her outdated coffee machine by the distinctive square of dust-free, stained countertop. I smiled to myself as I imagined where I would put my own machinery.

A spark of excitement came back as I contemplated what drinks to put on the menu. Unlike while I was working in an office full of uninitiated humans, in Willowmere I could proudly walk down the street with a cup of coffee that blew me steam kisses or changed colors with every sip. For once in my life, I could truly let my imagination run free.

"So this is where you ran off to, Clove."

Ice flooded through my veins, and my smile died a quick and painful death. I slowly turned to face the front door, and mentally kicked myself for not locking it behind me. I hadn't thought I'd need to here.

Leaning against the doorframe stood the absolute last person I wanted to see right now. The morning sun gilded the edges of his ginger hair but cast his icy blue eyes in shadow. Instead of his usual hoodie and jeans, today he wore a tailored tunic and trousers, with his grimoire attached to his leather belt. A smile curved his generous lips, but it didn't quite reach his cold eyes.

Schooling my face into a mask of cool indifference, I asked, "What are *you* doing in Willowmere, Rasmus? I was under the impression this place was far too much of a *backwoods town* for such an exalted potions master like yourself?"

"I came to get *you,* of course. You ran off before I had a chance to explain things." His voice took on that condescending tone I hated.

"Things seemed quite self-explanatory to me." The memory was seared into my mind.

"Nyssa was only helping me with—"

"I have absolutely *no* desire to learn what she was *helping* you with," I cut him off coldly. "I have a lot of work to get done, and no time to chat. There's the door; I trust you can see yourself out."

"I *did* hear a ridiculous rumor that you'd purchased this rickety old tear-down." Rasmus' lip curled as he glanced around at my pride and joy. How I had ever fantasized about kissing those lips now baffled me.

"Word travels fast," I muttered. It had only been, what? An hour? Two?

"I'm sure there's some loophole where you can get a full refund if you tell that centaur you've changed your mind. We can still put a down payment on that apartment you liked so much." He took a few steps towards me.

I resisted the urge to take a few steps back. "Too little, too late. I'm no longer even remotely interested in cohabitating with you."

"Don't be like that, Clover," he crooned, using his pet nickname for me. "If you're really that set on running your little business here, we can make it work. I'll even help you create an inspired new drink menu."

I gritted my teeth. "Don't call me that." He always did this; changing strategies until he got what he wanted, and eventually convincing me to do what *he* wanted instead of what *I* wanted. "And I don't need anyone's help to come up with the menu."

He raised his eyebrows, lifting his hands in a fake gesture of acceptance. "Alright, if that's what you want. But are you really sure you don't want the help of a *real* potions master?" His tone dripped with fake honey.

"I don't need to be a potions master to make a decent cup of coffee." Were we really having this argument *again?!*

"Those machines the humans invented are cute and all, but they're no replacement for a real warlock's brew." He advanced another step, until only a handful of feet separated us.

"At least my espresso machine won't betray me." My voice wobbled, despite my best efforts to keep it steady. If only Silas were here; he would have chased him off with one swipe of his needle-sharp claws.

"A little commitment issue doesn't have to be the end of the world. Of us." Rasmus stepped right up into my personal space and reached out a hand as if to touch my face.

I slapped it away. "The only commitment I want now is to creating the perfect latte foam."

Rasmus' calm demeanor cracked. "What do you want, Clover? An apology? Some money? If that's what this is about—"

"I don't want your father's money, Rasmus. I want you out of my building, and out of my life." I glared at him, refusing to back down and let him walk all over me again.

A vein throbbed in his forehead, and wisps of flame flickered to life in his hair, like it always did whenever he was angry. "Is there someone else? Is that what this is about?"

"So what if there is?" I said impulsively. And then I panicked when Rasmus' expression darkened.

This was going to be a very short-lived, very painful lie. My magic skills were impressive, but even I couldn't conjure a boyfriend out of thin air.

"Anyone I know?" There was a dangerous edge to his voice, the one he always got right before he did something he shouldn't.

"I—" I started, my voice failing me. What should I do? Should I just admit that I was lying? But then I would never hear the end of it!

The shadows shivered a moment before I heard footsteps on the stairs behind me. "About earlier, I wanted to—" The shadowmancer drew up short when he saw Rasmus, his violet eyes flicking between us and narrowing.

At least he was fully dressed this time. He wore an ocean blue, collared shirt with buttons that ran down the front, with a pair of black pants and shoes that only added to the impression that he was a part of the shadows that seemed to constantly waft from his tanned skin.

With lethal grace, he stepped up beside me. "Am I interrupting something?"

Before I even knew what I was doing, I wrapped my arm around the shadowmancer's and blurted out, "This is my new boyfriend."

Whose name I didn't even know. To his credit, the man hardly even blinked at my sudden clinginess and declaration.

Rasmus looked shocked for a moment, but he quickly recovered. "What is he, an actor? There's no way *you* of all people could—"

"The name's Thorne." The shadowmancer seemed to be taking this ridiculous situation in stride, and even held out his hand to Rasmus.

So his name was Thorne. That seemed oddly fitting for the shadowmancer.

Rasmus looked at his scarred and callused hand like it might bite him. "Rasmus." He hesitantly shook hands with the shadowmancer, and I could tell from his grimace that the man had a brutal grip.

I tried not to smile.

The shadowmancer was cool, calm, and convincing—and more than a little intimidating when he was glowering. At least this time, that glower wasn't directed at *me.* Rasmus sized him up, and seemed nervous at what he saw.

"Now, Rasmus, my lovely girlfriend and I were just about to start scrubbing the floor. Lots of old food and whatnot that needs to be chipped off. Care to lend us a hand?" Somehow, he even managed to make his smile look threatening.

"M-Maybe another time. I have...another appointment," Ramsus stammered quickly. Glancing at me, he added, "I'll be in town for a while—I'll make sure to stop by some other time to continue our...*discussion.*"

And with that, Rasmus scurried out of the shop.

I breathed a sigh of relief, some of the pent-up tension finally leaving my shoulders. Which was when I became acutely aware that I was still holding onto Thorne's very solid bicep, and that there was an inscrutable expression in his violet eyes as he peered down at me.

Chapter Four

Pumpkins & Pretending

Clove

I abruptly released his arm, my cheeks flaming. "Thank you. For playing along back there."

Thorne ran a hand through his dark hair. "Your ex?"

"Yes." I bit my lip. "He hates Willowmere. I never imagined he'd follow me all the way here."

Thorne's gaze sharpened, and his shadow flickered agitatedly. "Is he stalking you?"

"I...I don't think so," I answered slowly, feeling oddly touched that this near-stranger was showing me such concern. "But it *does* worry me that he plans to be in town for a while.

He's not the type to take time off of his precious job in Seattle to spend time in a small town—and especially not just to chase *me*."

"You think he's here on business."

I blinked, surprised he could tell what I was thinking so accurately. "I do. Which means I won't be able to get rid of him unless I turn him into a frog or something."

Thorne raised one eyebrow. "You can do that?"

"Theoretically." I sighed. "He's a lawyer by day, a potions master by night. He would sniff out that particular potion in a heartbeat. Unfortunately."

His lips curved in a slight smile. "Is that what you were about to do to me? When you barged in on me?"

I flushed at the reminder of our initial meeting. "No! That was a pixie banishment spell. In my defense, Mr. Chevalier failed to disclose that there was someone living in the apartment—sanctioned or otherwise."

"The desperate tend to leave out inconvenient details." His tone took on a hard edge that made me wonder what experience had caused it.

"Very true." My tone was only a shade lighter than his.

But now, I found myself in quite the pickle. I had no apartment *or* boyfriend—and Rasmus thought I had both. I wanted to avoid giving him the satisfaction of catching me in the lie at all costs. Even if I had to swallow my pride and ask for help from a complete stranger.

Clearing my throat, I pivoted to fully face Thorne. "How would you like to make a deal?"

"What kind of deal?" he asked warily, crossing his arms over his chest. I tried not to admire the way his sleeves pulled taut around his biceps.

"Evidently, you need a place to stay. And I need a boyfriend—at least until Rasmus returns to Seattle, which I imagine won't take more than a month, at most. So, in exchange for staying here rent free, will you pretend to be my boyfriend until the end of the Masquerade Ball?"

"Will you turn me into a frog if I refuse?" He looked serious, but a smile tugged at the corner of his mouth.

Was he *teasing* me?

"I just might." I wiggled my fingers, calling up a cleaning spell to glitter at my fingertips threateningly.

Though if I were being honest, I highly doubted I could do anything at all to him. Something about the way he held himself told me he was not unfamiliar with combat, magical or otherwise. Not to mention those scars all over his body...

"Well, I certainly can't have that." He gazed at me for an uncomfortably long moment, before he seemed to come to a decision. "Make it three months of rent, and I accept your terms, Miss...?"

I flushed, realizing belatedly that I had yet to tell him my name. "Morelli. Clove Morelli."

I held out my hand for him to shake, which he did—far more gently than he must have with Rasmus.

"So, Miss Morelli. What do you plan on doing with this building now that it's yours?" His voice was distractingly deep.

"Just Clove is fine. I used to love spending time in this café when I was little, and I want others to be able to enjoy it too. But cooking is not my forte, so instead, I thought I'd open a coffee shop!" I grinned. "I already have the name and color scheme picked out, and I have plenty of ideas for magically-infused drinks to add to the menu, and—"

"I see you've given this a lot of thought." His gaze was appraising.

"More than you can imagine," I said softly.

"What are we doing first, then? Cleaning?" Thorne began to carefully roll us his sleeves, exposing his muscled forearms and dark tattoos I had failed to notice before. They wrapped around his arms in a series of elegant swirls and intricate patterns.

"Wait, *we?* You're going to help me?" I had been so distracted that I nearly didn't notice what he'd said.

"What kind of fake boyfriend would I be if I let my girlfriend do all the heavy lifting?"

"Are you sure? Not that I wouldn't appreciate the help, but we would only need to act like a couple in public." I bit my lip.

Didn't Thorne have better things to do with his time? From what I had heard, shadowmancers were relatively rare, and were therefore always in high demand as adventurers.

"And what were you planning on telling Rasmus if he popped back in and you were alone?" His quiet question rattled me.

If Thorne hadn't appeared when he did, would Rasmus really have taken no for an answer? Even though we had dated for two years, I wasn't entirely positive he would not have tried to take me back by force.

"You're not too busy?" I summoned the mop into my hands.

His expression softened a fraction. "My schedule is wide open."

"Great!" I shoved the mop at him with a mischievous grin. "Then you can start with the floors."

He exhaled in a way that sounded suspiciously like a laugh, but made no complaints. Instead, he immediately got to work, and I had to tear my gaze away from the way his muscles bunched with the movement.

Then I gave myself a mental shake. After Rasmus, I think I needed a long break from emotional entanglements—no matter how tall, dark, and broody they may appear.

Refocusing on the task at hand, I fired off spells left and right, dusting here and polishing there. The windows were soon sparkling clean and most of the dust and cobwebs were taken care of. Though for some reason, Thorne was doing the mopping by hand, instead of using his shadows to do it for him.

Now that the interior was looking so much better, I wandered into the back storage room to see if that needed cleaning. It was a small, cramped room, with metal rolling shelves that lined each wall and were packed with cardboard boxes.

With a wave of my hand, I fired off a handful of cleaning spells to get to work while I investigated the boxes. Mrs. Virgil had been meticulous in her labeling, so I quickly learned that the boxes towards the front contained various tools and kitchen supplies, the ones in the middle held things like chalk for the menu board and umbrellas for the tables outside, and the ones towards the back held seasonal decorations.

Perfect—some Halloween decorations were just what the place needed to brighten it up.

Unfortunately, the Halloween box was on the top shelf and just out of reach. I went onto my toes and stretched up to try and reach the box, but my fingertips just barely brushed the cardboard edge. Changing tactics, I used a spell to pull the box towards the edge, though it seemed to be a bit heavier than I was expecting.

For a moment, it teetered on the edge before gravity made its claim and pulled it into the open air. Which was when I realized the box was far larger and heavier than I initially thought—and it was headed straight for my face.

"Watch out!"

Soft shadows wrapped around my hips like a vine, before yanking me back against a hard chest as strong arms tightened around me. Before I could react, the box I had been trying to reach crashed down exactly where I had been standing a moment before. A dust cloud ballooned, causing my eyes to start watering, and tiny plastic pumpkins scattered all over the floor.

"Did we not just agree you would let *me* do the heavy lifting?" His voice rumbled in his chest, making me suddenly, acutely aware Thorne was still holding me rather protectively.

Color rose in my cheeks as I peeked up at him. "I didn't realize it was that heavy. Thank you."

"You're...welcome." He almost sounded shocked that I had thanked him.

Am I interrupting something? Silas intoned in my mind.

I jumped, looking around frantically. I hadn't just accidentally squashed my own familiar, had I?

"What's wrong?" Thorne's arms tightened for a moment before he released me.

"Silas is here!"

"Silas?" His eyes narrowed. "How many boyfriends do you have?"

I sagged with relief as I spotted my cat's form slinking into the room and scooped him up in my arms. I rolled my eyes and laughed. "Silas is my familiar, silly."

The line of his tensed shoulders relaxed as he peered at my cat. "Oh." He reached out a hand to pet him, but after Silas sniffed it, he hissed at him.

He reeks of blood and darkness. His pupils slitted. *Why is he here?*

A chill ran down my spine.

"I'm so sorry about him; my familiar has no manners," I said aloud as Thorne withdrew his hand. Silently, I asked Silas, *What do you mean?*

Instead of answering, he wriggled free from my arms and leaped onto one of the shelves to watch us both from a higher vantage point.

"Are you at least going to help?" I asked aloud for Thorne's benefit.

A single pumpkin decoration magically rolled back into the crumpled remains of the box. And then Silas began to groom himself.

"Gee, thanks." I propped my hands on my hips. "Whatever would I do without you?"

With a snap of my fingers, I repaired the box and sent all of the little pumpkin decorations back in with a wave of my hand. When I glanced at Thorne, he was watching me with a hint of amusement behind his violet eyes.

"Would you mind?" I asked sheepishly, gesturing at the box.

"Not at all." With an ease I envied, he scooped up the box like it was filled with feathers.

I led the way back into the shop, and he placed the box down gently on top of one of the freshly-polished countertops. I grabbed my grimoire from where it hung from my belt and flipped it open to the middle. After consulting it on the verbiage, I invented a charm on the spot to levitate and attach all of the decorations in the box throughout the space.

After gathering my magic power and muttering the words, all of the cute little decorations danced out of the box and swirled through the air until I could direct each one to where I wanted it. I hung the purple curtains over the windows, draped the pumpkin lights along the walls, and arranged the fake Jack o'Lanterns along the counters and in the corners of the room. Then I sent all of the fake candles to hover in the air near the ceiling.

That took a bit more magic than I had anticipated, so I leaned against the counter as I wiped my brow. I would need to refine that charm so that it used less energy in the future.

"Did you just create a new spell?" Thorne looked impressed.

I nodded. "Nothing fancy, just a simple charm. It eats up a bit too much magic for my liking though, so I'll have to refine it before I use it again."

"You do know it takes most witches weeks to do what you just did in a few minutes, right?" he asked.

"It does?" My mom always rattled off new charms like it was nothing, and Rasmus had never batted an eye at the practice, either.

"It does." Thorne gave me an inscrutable look. "After all of that hard work, how about I take you out for lunch?"

I blinked. "What?"

"We should also discuss our public appearances as a couple." He smirked, crossing his arms.

"Good idea. And I could definitely go for an iced coffee right about now. I'm happy to treat you, though," I added quickly. "As thanks for your help."

He frowned for a moment, before understanding dawned in his eyes. "I'm only squatting in the apartment because I was turned away from the inn and the realtor's office, not because I couldn't pay."

Now it was my turn to frown. "Why would they not accept your business? And why did you ask for three months of free rent, then?!"

His expression hardened. "Shadowmancers have...something of a reputation. Though only the older generation can tell what I am unless I use my powers." After a moment of silence, his eyes softened. "Why not ask? You agreed, after all."

"I suppose I did, didn't I?" I pushed off from the counter and led the way to the front entrance. Silas, the little nuisance, appeared to trot along at my feet, no doubt summoned by the mention of food. After I had locked the door behind me, it suddenly occurred to me to ask, "How did you get in without a key?"

Thorne grinned. "Shadowmancers make excellent lockpicks. There are very few locks that can keep us out." He held up a key that was identical to mine but made out of solidified shadows.

I laughed, shaking my head. "I'm sure that little trick comes in handy."

"Very. Shall we? I hear The Hearthstone Diner makes an excellent coffee." Thorne offered me his arm, and after a moment of hesitation, I took it.

"I will be the judge of that. I was trained by a true Italian master, I will have you know, so I have very high standards."

"I don't doubt it," he commented, his violet eyes seeming to see right through me.

And for some reason, I don't think he was still referencing coffee.

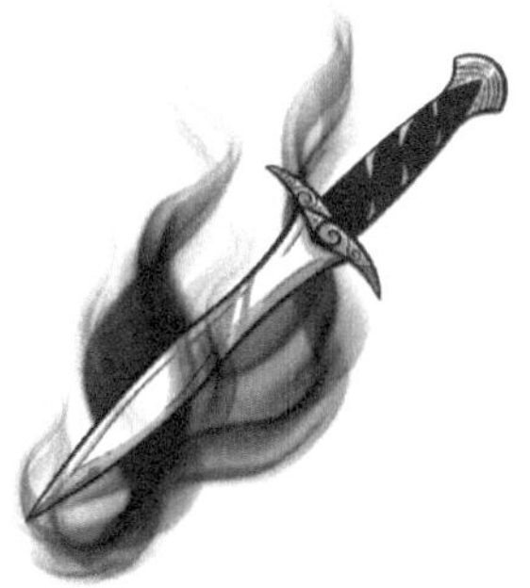

CHAPTER FIVE

Witches & Wonders

THORNE

Well, wonders never ceased.

How did I go from moping around in my kitchen to having a stunning witch sitting across from me in a very public diner in a matter of hours?

Even though I had been in Willowmere for a while, I had hardly set foot inside any of its establishments. I only knew that the fifties-themed diner with red vinyl booths was popular thanks to the conversations my shadows had overheard in town. Apparently, it was run by fire drakes, but only one of the

45

waitresses here bore the telltale horns and trademark red hair of their kind.

I watched Clove over the rim of my cup of tea. She made a face every time she took a sip of her coffee, so I guess she hadn't been joking about being a coffee connoisseur.

"You don't have to drink it," I commented drily, amused.

She glanced around before pushing the mug away from her. "Now I see why Mr. Chevalier expected my coffee shop to do well." Her eyes met mine before darting away again. "And why he was so eager to sell the building."

"Sounds like he's been having a hard time getting some sucker to take it off his hands."

"Are you calling me a sucker?" Clove glared at me, crossing her arms over her chest. "And anyways, whose fault do you think *that* is?!"

I shrugged. Took a sip of my tea. Dumped another two lumps of sugar into it. Took another sip. Nope, still tasted terrible.

"Hopefully the food is better than the drinks," I muttered, flagging down our waitress.

The nagas, or snake-woman, slithered over to us. "Are you ready to placcce your ordersss?"

"Yes. I would like to try the Dragonfire Dumplings with a side of fries." If they weren't overcooked, I would consider myself lucky.

"And I would like the Inferno Noodles," Clove added.

Once our waitress slithered away, I found myself scanning the diner for the tenth time. Checking for threats, verifying the closest exits, and keeping an ear out for raised voices or sudden whispers.

"Is something wrong?" Clove asked, brow furrowing.

Yes. *Me.*

You could take me out of the dungeons, but you couldn't take the dungeon-bred alertness out of me.

"No, everything's fine." I cleared my throat. "So, how would you like to go about this? It might be wise to tell me your boundaries, and a little bit about yourself so that we can pull this off convincingly."

Clove nodded once, twice. "Of course. And thank you again for agreeing to help me with this." She blushed before continuing. "Public displays of affection are required, but I will be staying with my parents until your three months of free rent are up. As for me, well... I recently left my...boyfriend, Rasmus and quit my finance job in Seattle—in the human side of the city—and have moved back into my childhood room, which I thought I had left behind for good when I went off to college."

"Understood." There was clearly more to the story than that, but I decided not to push her on it just yet. "How frequently would you like me to take you on public dates?"

Clove tapped her chin as she thought. "Two or three times a week, depending on how long it takes me to get the shop ready for business."

I swallowed. Two or three times a week felt like a lot after avoiding going outside the apartment, except for groceries and necessities for the last year. But then I gave myself a mental shake. Here was my chance to finally fill a fraction of the loneliness that had been plaguing me for so long; I was not about to let it pass me by.

"What's your favorite color?" I asked abruptly.

"Violet—like your eyes." Clove blushed and looked down, as if she hadn't meant to add that last part.

I was saved from answering when Nalini, our waitress, set two steaming plates in front of us. "Enjoy."

I could practically feel the spice radiating from the dumplings. It seemed the rumor that fire drakes liked their food spicy was true, after all. One bite in, and I was already wishing I had ordered some milk. I took a few more bites, watching as Clove did the same. Her turquoise eyes were soon watering.

Before mine could follow suit, I flagged Nalini down again. "We'll take two chocolate milkshakes, as well."

She smirked at me. "Coming right up, sssir."

"How did you know I like chocolate?" Clove was clearly trying not to cough.

"Since you like coffee, and probably mochas, I figured I couldn't go wrong with another chocolate beverage."

"Thanks." Clove gave me a tentative smile, which I returned with a nod.

When our shakes arrived, I think we both ended up sucking down about half of them in one gulp.

"My favorite color is blue, by the way. Though I think I might have a soft spot for turquoise," I told her quietly.

This time, her blush reached her ears.

CHAPTER SIX

Cinnamon & Cider

CLOVE

"Hold still," Thorne murmured, as he leaned in close. His breath smelled like cinnamon, which he had sprinkled generously on his mocha this morning. He seemed to like it so much that I had decided to add it to the menu.

My heartbeat sped up, despite my best efforts to keep it calm, and despite the knowledge that we were simply putting on a show. He came close enough that I could see the flecks of silver in his violet eyes. Thorne's fingers brushed through the strands of my long hair as he removed the crimson leaf that was caught there.

"Thank you." I plastered on a smile as he laced his fingers through mine while we continued our stroll down main street.

Our acting had the desired effect; the young ladies sitting under The Hearthstone Diner's patio umbrellas giggled and whispered behind their hands as we passed.

Though it had only been two days since we made our bargain, news of our "relationship" had already spread through town like a magical tidal wave.

And apparently, the residents of Willowmere were downright *delighted*.

Even my parents had caught wind of it. They were justifiably horrified, considering the reason I had moved back home in the first place, but once I explained the situation, they were both fairly understanding.

So far, the hardest part of this whole charade was getting used to Thorne's presence. He tended to make about as much noise as a shadow, and kept popping up out of nowhere throughout the day. But after his initial hesitation, he had become much more confident with the public displays of affection.

I had also managed to convince Thorne to accompany me to the Moonlit Masquerade Ball as my partner. That hadn't been easy, however, considering the shadowmancer seemed to be allergic to most forms of fun, and dancing in particular.

When we reached the door to The Broom & Bean, he held it open for me like a true gentleman. And here I'd thought that chivalry was dead. Even my former fiancé had rarely done things like that.

It seemed my fake boyfriend was far more attentive than my real one ever had been.

The space was finally starting to look like a coffee shop. It was all nice and clean, and I'd salvaged what I could of the furniture. With the help of Thorne and his shadows, I had rearranged everything so that there was one main counter, and the rest of the space was laid out like an inviting living room.

The tables were mismatched on purpose—each one salvaged, sanded, and enchanted with small personality quirks. One purred when you set down your mug; another adjusted its height depending on yours. The chairs were overstuffed, velvet-backed, and impossibly comfortable, as though they had been designed specifically for lingering conversations or curling up with a good book.

Soft paper lanterns, instead of fire-hazard candles, floated near the ceiling, gently drifting with the air currents, and casting warm gold and amber light across the room. A few enchanted pumpkins—glowing softly in seasonal oranges and yellows—sat in the corners, murmuring cheerful greetings when we entered. The fireplace now crackled with magical, smokeless fire, glowing in shades of red and gold, and warming the room with both heat and its peaceful ambiance.

"It's really coming along." Thorne moved to stand beside me.

I smiled happily. "Now I think I can start focusing on creating the menu." I glanced at the bare shelves behind the counter. "Though I'm going to need to purchase some supplies first."

"Hmm. If you're going to add seasonal drinks, I think I've heard of a good place to get some pumpkins and cinnamon. Plus, it's bound to be rather crowded this time of year—though I can't say for certain, as I haven't been before."

I gaped at him. "You've never been to a pumpkin patch before?"

His expression shuttered. "Until recently, I never had the time."

Keeping my curiosity in check, I opted not to pry, my mind flashing back to the scars I had seen on his chest. "In that case, I would be happy to give you the grand tour. The pumpkin patch is just outside of town, and owned by a dryad. It's a little unusual, compared to those in the human world, but that only makes it more fun. We can go together after I finish putting together Silas' cat tree."

"Sounds like a plan." The hint of a smile softened Thorne's expression. "Your familiar wants...a cat tree?"

Silas hissed from his spot on one of the armchairs. *You try being nearly sat on and see how* you *like it.*

"He has an irrational fear of people's rears after Rasmus accidentally sat on him. Hence he wants his own comfy spot all to himself," I translated.

You didn't have to tell him that *part.* Silas turned baleful eyes on me.

Your phrasing leaves much to be desired, I retorted.

With the utmost gravity, Thorne told Silas, "I agree that it is very important to have one's own space. It helps reduce the urge to take a swipe at people who bother you."

The cat's tail flicked back and forth. *See? He gets it.*

Yes, yes. You're both anti-social. I rolled my eyes. *I'll get to work.*

I crooked my finger at the box that had arrived this morning via the pegasus mail service, and it obediently slid over to me. A small slicing spell and levitation charm later, and the box was open and all of the parts were floating in the air in front of me.

"Would you like some help?" Thorne offered.

"Are you sure?" I still wasn't used to how freely he offered his help.

"I am." He gave me a wink. "How hard could it be? Besides, the sooner we get this done, the sooner I get my tour."

I laughed. "Alright then, let's get to work!"

Two botched attempts and four cat treats later, we had finally assembled the cat tree. It was three stories of scratching posts, ramps, and cushy lounging spots, but so far, Silas was far more interested in the box it came in.

"Will you at least try it out?" I asked him, exasperated after all that effort.

Maybe later. He watched me through half-open eyes from his loafing position in the box.

I rolled my eyes.

"So? Does he like it?" Thorne folded his arms over his chest.

"He's absolutely thrilled," I deadpanned. Shaking my head, I said, "Why don't we get ready to go to the pumpkin patch? Silas can explore it while we're gone."

"Then I will meet you there."

I arrived a little late, since I had spent longer than I wanted to admit selecting an outfit from my limited wardrobe back home. Why teenage me had worn nothing but short skirts and skinny jeans was now a complete mystery to me. Eventually, I had picked out a lovely chestnut-colored maxi skirt and cream sweater to wear, with my favorite soft leather boots.

I looked around for Thorne's distinctive silhouette, shading my eyes from the warm afternoon sunlight with my hand. But although there were a handful of other people milling about near the entrance, I didn't see him. Perhaps he was waiting for me inside. I started strolling along the main dirt path, reminiscing about my previous visits here.

The pumpkin patch was owned and lovingly tended by Thistle, a soft-spoken dryad with hair like trailing willow leaves and skin the hue of autumn bark. She spoke to her pumpkins in the old tongue of roots and rain, coaxing them to ripen in shades of dusky orange, moonlight white, and even the occasional pale lavender—kissed by her own unique enchantments. When I was little, I had been absolutely fascinated by her magic, which was so different from my own. But Thistle was a kind and patient spirit, and would answer every question I cared to come up with.

She took meticulous care of the property, which was obvious even at a glance. Winding vines stretched like lazy cats across the loamy soil, which was dotted with fat pumpkins beneath fan-like leaves. Unlike a regular pumpkin patch, the vines here prospered all year long.

Wooden archways draped in flowering ivy guided visitors along the winding footpaths, each marked with charming hand-carved signs: *Cinderella Pumpkins, Fairy Lantern Gourds, Cider Hollow*. A gentle breeze always seemed to carry the scent of cinnamon throughout the property, and hidden in the patch's corners were quaint gazebos and fountains. I had spent many a lazy afternoon reading in them, or tucked away in one of her cushioned swings.

"There you are." Thorne's low timbre echoed out from a shadowy archway.

"Don't do that!" My heart leaped out of my chest for a moment as he emerged from the darkness, looking striking in long pants and a dark, collared shirt. I could have sworn there was no one there a moment ago. Wait, unless… "Were you hiding in the shadows?"

"An occupational perk." His violet eyes skimmed over my outfit, and he took my hand, pressing a light kiss to the back of it. "You look lovely, by the way."

I flushed. "Don't change the subject."

Thorne looked down, seemingly chagrined. "Sorry. It's a habit. I promise I won't scare you again."

I noticed he hadn't promised not to sulk in the shadows again, but I supposed I should be happy with the compromise. "Thank you. And for the compliment—you look dashing as well."

Surprise flashed in his eyes. If he was *that* unused to compliments, I should make sure to slip them in more often.

"Thank you," he said hesitantly, before clearing his throat and offering his arm. "So, where are we going first on our tour?"

"I thought we could start by picking out a few fresh pumpkins to use as decorations for the shop." I slipped my arm through his, and started strolling down the path labeled, *Fairy Lantern Gourds.*

"*More* pumpkins?" His tone told me he thought we already had plenty in the shop.

"The fake ones are nice enough, but they're no replacement for the real deal. Besides, I wanted to get a few of the tastier ones so that I can add pumpkin spice lattes to the menu." I trailed my free hand along the flowers that lined the path.

"Are those lattes popular?" Thorne frowned. "I can't say that I've tried one before."

I stopped dead in my tracks. "Seriously?!"

The ghost of a smile curved his lips. "Seriously."

"I'll just have to make you one, then." I continued along the path. "Tell me you've at least tried a latte before."

Thorne studiously avoided my eyes. "Well…"

"I see I have my work cut out for me." A laugh bubbled up before I could stop it, and Thorne looked at me in surprise. "But fear not, I plan to make my Italian master proud. I'll have you singing the praises of espressos, lattes, and mochas alike before I'm through with you."

"I'll look forward to that." Thorne watched me with the strangest expression on his face, but it was gone before I could ask about it.

It suddenly occurred to me that I knew next to nothing about him. And he hardly knew much about me, either. If we were going to play convincing lovers, it would be a good idea to change that.

Our cover was most certainly the only reason. I was definitely *not* curious about the shadowmancer and his mysterious past.

Once we turned the final corner, the pumpkin patch lay spread out in front of us. Rows of pumpkins of all different shapes and colors were scattered artfully across the field. Some were short and round, while others were tall and bulbous. As we walked down one row, I pointed out to Thorne how some looked like they were made of glitter or glass, and some changed colors every few seconds. A few had already been claimed by forest sprites, with little doors and windows carved into them and smoke puffing out of their chimney-like stems.

"I didn't know there were so many magical varieties," Thorne murmured, his gaze riveted to a purple pumpkin that shimmered with hints of blue and green.

"How about we each pick out three?" I suggested. "Two for the shop and one to keep?"

"In that case..." With a wink, Thorne wandered off, heading for that purple one.

I scanned the patch as well. The first pumpkin I picked was a classic orange, with a golden filigree that shifted designs every few breaths. For my second, I selected the glass one I had spotted earlier, already planning to give it pride of place on the shop's countertop, next to the register. And for my third one, I decided on a dark pumpkin that almost looked like it was carved from darkness, with glimmers of silver and violet light that reminded me of a starry night sky...and a certain someone's eyes.

I levitated my selection and had them trail behind me like the tail of a kite. Somehow, Thorne was walking towards me with three pumpkins balanced in his arms. One was the shimmery purple one that matched my usual dress, one looked like it was made of an ocean wave, and the third looked for all the world like a cloud of smoke shaped into the vague form of a pumpkin, and carried the faint scent of apple and cinnamon.

"You picked some great ones." I nodded approvingly at his armful.

"As did you." His eyes lingered a beat too long on the shadowy pumpkin.

"Let's take them to Thistle—she'll hold them for us in the back until we're ready to leave." I glanced at him askance. "Aren't you going to use your shadows to carry those? Or do you want me to levitate them for you?"

"Thank you, but I can manage." When I looked at him questioningly, he lowered his voice and explained, "Keeping a low profile, remember?"

I nodded, and led the way to the quaint little barn that housed Thistle's shop, which was packed with seeds and knick-knacks for sale. There was a lilac-haired fae girl managing the till.

"I love your hair color," I complimented her, as I handed over my pumpkins, and Thorne did the same.

"Thank you. You two make a lovely couple, by the way." She beamed at me, showing off her sharp canines, and twirled a lock of hair around her finger. Leaning in like she was about to share a secret, she whispered, "I recommend heading over to the cider house soon—they tend to run out around four o'clock."

"Thanks for the tip. We'll head there first before we visit the maze." Without thinking, I grabbed Thorne's hand and towed him towards the cider house before he could see the blush on my cheeks.

At least our ruse was working.

The cider house was packed when we got there. All of the tables that crowded the inside of the building were taken, and there was even a line at the counter to order. Two dryads were busily preparing the drinks, and another two were handing out freshly-made apple cider donuts, which were covered in cinnamon sugar. We quickly hopped in line, and I enjoyed taking deep breaths of the warm, spice-laden air.

"I think she told that secret to everyone," Thorne murmured against the shell of my ear, sending shivers down my spine.

"Looks that way," I answered. "Though the cider is always popular this time of year."

"Maybe we should add it to the menu, then."

I loved the way he said *we*.

My sense of contentment evaporated the moment I heard the person ahead of me in line speak. I stiffened, and instinctively took a step back—right into Thorne. He steaded me with a hand at my waist, his gaze immediately snapping up, as if to scan for threats.

"What's wrong?"

"Those are Rasmus' parents ahead of us in line," I whispered so quietly my lips barely moved. For a fleeting moment, I seriously considered beating a hasty retreat.

"Do you want to leave?" There wasn't so much as a hint of judgment or censure in his tone.

I was tempted. But wouldn't that defeat the purpose of my arrangement with Thorne? "No."

Thorne's eyes lit with wicked amusement, and he leaned down to whisper against my ear, "Then how about we put on a little show for them?"

I almost protested. *Almost.* But then I remembered their disapproving stares at every dinner I'd had the misfortune of sitting through at their table. "Let's make it good."

To my surprise, Thorne then tightened his grip on my waist, pulling me flush against him, and delicately grasped my chin. His violet eyes dropped to my lips a moment before he claimed my mouth with his.

At first, his lips were gentle, searching. He teased my mouth with caresses while his thumb stroked slow circles on my lower back. But then, his kisses became more urgent, more demanding. The scent of cinnamon mixed with his own scent of pine in a heady combination that wreathed my senses.

I practically swooned.

My eyelids fluttered shut as he caressed my lips, and I wrapped my arms around his neck, tangling my fingers in his dark hair. I was enjoying myself so much that I didn't even want to come up for air.

But when I heard an odd, strangled noise next to us, my eyes snapped open. Thorne gave me a lazy grin that set butterflies loose in my stomach.

"Clove?!" gasped my former mother-in-law to be. "What on earth are you doing? You're engaged to my son!"

It would seem Rasmus hadn't even told his parents yet. Was *that* why he had come all the way to Willowmere? To win me back before they found out what he'd done?

I smiled. That option was now off the table for Rasmus. Hopefully, that meant he would leave me alone now.

"Didn't you hear, Bellatrix? The wedding's off." I was proud of how steady my voice was.

"What? When? Why?!" Her face pinched in confusion and outrage.

"Ask your liar of a son," I said, before turning to Thorne. "Let's get out of here. Something smells sour."

I turned on my heel and left, hand-in-hand with Thorne, leaving Bellatrix to sputter indignantly behind us.

CHAPTER SEVEN

Lattes & Longing

THORNE

Wow.

Just wow.

At first, I had only intended to humor Clove's request, and to get myself a few more months of peace before moving on to the next magical town. But that kiss was just...

Wow.

Sure, I had dated occasionally before, but I had never felt such immediate chemistry with anyone. And I had never had anyone react to *me* like that, either.

And here I was worried that I'd gotten rusty.

My lips curved up in a smile, and I had to resist the urge to touch them. I lay back on my bed, my gaze automatically finding the window and the stars that glittered in the night. I could hardly remember the last time I had smiled this much. Or the last time walking around town in broad daylight had felt so...comfortable.

When I was alone, it always felt like I was being glared at by the townsfolk. It made me feel vulnerable, being out in the open with no one to guard my back. But when I went out with Clove, the glances that came my way weren't hostile at all.

Except, of course, for the parents of her ex-boyfriend. I could hardly even picture their faces; I had been far too focused on Clove to pay them much attention. But I was glad she had seemed so satisfied with the looks on their faces.

It was inspiring to see her confront her own fears like that. Unlike me, she refused to run from her problems; she faced them head on.

I had known plenty of adventurers in my time who had less of a backbone than one little witch.

But that was just a part of her charm, of what made her so special.

I groaned, and rested my arm over my eyes. The light of the stars was far too bright, just like how Clove's brilliance was far too dazzling for a reclusive shadowmancer like me.

She was dangerous, this witch. Dangerous in an entirely unexpected way.

After all, I was meant to be leaving Willowmere in three months. Getting too attached would only end up making things harder. Hurting Clove was the last thing I wanted to do. Besides, I had a feeling that Clove shedding a single tear would result in Silas taking a few swipes at me.

I snorted, remembering the faint lines I had noticed on Rasmus' arms when I first met him. It didn't take a genius to figure out where *those* had come from. I'd have to remember to reward the feline with some tasty treats for his excellent aim the next time I saw him.

Rasmus, on the other hand... I didn't like how possessive he had been acting towards Clove. And after that show we put on in front of his parents... His pride must have taken quite the hit.

I summoned two of my shadow soldiers, who knelt at my bedside. *What is your command?*

One of you will guard the witch's home. The other will guard the shop downstairs.

What is the nature of the threat?

One warlock, though I would not put it past him to recruit help. It never hurt to be prepared. *Guard against spellwork from a distance, as well.*

Understood. We will eliminate the warlock if he dares—

No, I interrupted him. *You are not to kill him. Your orders are to defend, not to attack. If the warlock's attacks persist, alert me or incapacitate him without causing permanent injury.*

A prideful warlock like Rasmus would only become more enraged with a severe injury. Besides, I doubted Clove would have wanted that. After all, Silas only scratched him. If she had wanted, Clove probably could have made life much more difficult for him.

No, she clearly wanted to move on, and that would be difficult if her ex insisted on hanging around.

We will not kill. Only defend, My soldiers' voices rasped in my mind.

Good. Report any attacks immediately.

As you wish, my lord. The two soldiers dissolved into shadow and streaked away. One attached itself to the darkness beneath Clove's bedroom window, while the other gazed out of the shadowy recesses of a carved pumpkin on the shop's doorstep downstairs.

Rolling onto my side, I let out a sigh. At least now, I would have a bit more peace of mind. I closed my eyes, and let thoughts of turquoise waters lull me to sleep.

Morning light played across my eyelids, dragging me up from the comforting depths of sleep. With a groan, I flicked a hand and threw up a wall of shadow across the window. I must have forgotten to close the curtains last night.

My brows furrowed. Why was that? I had been looking at the stars, and thinking about how their light reminded me of something... Or was it someone?

A machine roared to life in the shop down below my borrowed apartment. Why Clove loved that noisy espresso machine so much was a mystery to me.

I sat bolt upright in bed. Clove! She must be working on creating new recipes for her menu. Which meant I could be spending time with her right now.

I let my curtain of darkness fall away as I wiped the sleep out of my eyes. Grabbing some fresh clothes, I made my way over to the bathroom so I could take my morning shower.

This time, I made sure to lock the door behind me.

I kept my shower brief, using the time to check in with my shadow soldiers. The one stationed at Clove's home reported that nothing had been out of the ordinary all night, which was good to hear.

But the one I had positioned at the shop's entrance related how Rasmus had stumbled over to the shop in the early hours of the morning. Evidently, the warlock had attempted to cast some sort of hex on the door, but had slurred his words so badly that the incantation hadn't activated the spell. And then, he had tripped his way back to wherever he was staying.

I scowled. Sometimes, I hated when I was right. At least, based on my soldier's description, Rasmus had been so drunk that he likely wouldn't remember his little attempt at vandalism.

I was doubly glad I had thought to station guards at both locations. Even though his revenge had failed, it was good to know what sort of petty person we were dealing with.

Should I station a soldier in Clove's shadow, just to be safe? No, that felt far too invasive of her privacy, even if I only meant to protect her. I suppose that meant I just needed to stay by her side as much as I could when she wasn't at home or at the shop.

Yes, that was the only reason. I didn't have any ulterior motives, like wanting to feel her hand in mine or inhale the scent of coffee and magic that seemed to waft from her soft skin.

I turned off the hot water and welcomed the bracing downpour of cold water. After a few minutes of that, I turned it off completely and quickly toweled dry before dressing for the day.

As soon as I opened the apartment's front door, the aroma of coffee hit me full-force. I smiled to myself as I jogged down the stairs. Sure enough, Clove was standing in front of her espresso machine, and fiddling with the milk frothing wand.

On silent feet, I padded up behind her until I could look over her shoulder. I watched as she artfully poured the steaming milk into two mugs of coffee. But instead of just dumping the milk in like I would have done, she moved the milk jug back and forth. The trail of milk started forming a pattern against the dark brown of the coffee.

It took me a minute to figure out what the design was. By the time she finished making the latte art for the second mug and set it down on the counter, I was grinning.

"Is that a witch hat?" I asked, my voice lower and more gravelly than usual thanks to the early hour.

Clove jumped, but I steadied her with a hand at her waist. She turned to me with wide eyes and put a hand over her heart.

"Thorne! I told you not to pop out of nowhere like that, didn't I?" she chided, her breathy voice sending warmth straight to my core.

"Sorry. Old habits." I reluctantly removed my hand from her waist and ran it through my hair. Wait, had I combed it after I got out of the shower? For the life of me, I couldn't remember.

Clove's fingers twitched as she stared at my probably messy hair. She cleared her throat and turned to grab one of the mugs, which she then held out to me. "Here."

"Thank you." My fingers brushed hers as I took the mug. Its warmth instantly seeped into my hand, and I held it up for a closer look at the design. "This *is* one of those pointy witch hats, right?"

"That's right." Clove smiled as she took a sip from her own mug, and sighed contentedly. "They may be out of style now, but my mom still likes to wear hers on special occasions."

"You're very artistic." I took a sip while trying not to mess up the design.

"Thank you." Her eyes dropped to her mug, but I saw the way the tips of her ears turned pink.

"You could definitely add this to the menu—it could be The Broom & Bean's signature drink," I suggested. "I bet people will love it."

"You think so?" Clover perked up. "Maybe I will! Though I think I'll have to add in a dash of magic. Maybe something that will allow the drinker to create a shower of sparkles from their fingertips?"

"That is a brilliant idea! As long as the sparkles have no sparks in them; you wouldn't want teenagers running around causing fires everywhere they went." I smirked at the mental image.

"Good point," Clove said with a chuckle.

We leaned against the counter, side by side, as we sipped our drinks. I felt more relaxed than I had in a long time. The silence was a comfortable one. I could imagine myself spending many more mornings just like this.

"Would you like some fruit? Kana will be bringing over pastries later, but I thought you might be hungry..." Clove trailed off as she glanced at the bowl of fruit on the counter just in time to watch the last banana transform into a fish and float straight towards Silas, who was perched on top of one of the armchairs instead of his cat tree.

"Silas! What are you doing?!" Clove gasped, setting down her mug with a sharp *clack*.

Clove paused for a beat, then frowned and retorted, "What do you mean, you were hungry? I just fed you breakfast an hour ago!"

I chuckled, and took one last sip of my latte before setting it aside. Even though I could only hear one side of their conversation, I could guess how the feline was responding. Clove glared at her familiar, but I wasn't entirely sure if they were still conversing mentally.

After a minute, I cleared my throat. "Clove, how about I go and pick up a few groceries while you add those sparkles to the recipe?"

"Thanks, Thorne. That would be a big help. We could use some more milk and fruit, since *someone* ate them all—and some of the magical herbs and ingredients on the list by the fridge."

"You got it," I said, grabbing the paper list and quickly scanning it. "I'll be back before the shadows shift."

CHAPTER EIGHT

Whispers & Warnings

CLOVE

"**W**hy didn't you tell me you were back in town?!" Kana squealed, tackling me in a hug. "I shouldn't have had to find out my bestie was here from the old ladies gossiping about the scene you made in the cider line yesterday!"

Though it had been over a year since I'd last seen her, my old friend looked the same as I remembered. Blue eyes sparkled in her heart-shaped face, and her fluffy fox ears blended in seamlessly with her silvery-blonde hair. She wore a cute sweater and skirt that allowed her three fox tails to swish freely behind her, tempting Silas to pounce with every flick.

At least my familiar had *finally* deigned to use his new cat tree—though only after I had thrown out the box it came in.

"Sorry, Kana! Things have been so hectic lately that I can hardly remember my own name sometimes," I explained with an apologetic grin.

Over a steaming cup of my latest coffee creation, which changed flavors with every sip, and some scones Kana brought me, I proceeded to tell her all about why I had come back to Willowmere, including how I had bought the building and my current arrangement with its sole tenant. She scowled and beamed at all the right places, and it was such a relief to get everything off of my chest.

"So where is this mysterious man of shadows?" Kana made a point of looking around my now perfectly-decorated coffee shop.

I laughed. "Thorne is picking up a few groceries for me this morning—I already have the supplies I need for the more typical drinks I plan to offer, but I want to experiment with some of my more seasonal and magical creations."

Kana gave me a knowing look. "You can let your creativity shine here, unlike back in that stuffy office full of humans."

"Very true." I sighed ruefully. "I think I'm starting to realize that making a name for myself among the humans was never really *my* dream. It was Rasmus', and my parents'. I was never truly happy while I was chasing it."

Kana placed her hand over mine. "At least you figured that out before you married that flaming douzledorf."

"Figured out what?" Thorne asked as he came in the front door, a canvas tote bag filled with groceries on one arm.

Kana's mouth made a perfect little *o* as she drank him in. She then gave me a grin I could only describe as foxy. I lightly kicked her foot under the table before she could say anything impulsive.

She winked at me. "How good Clove is at making lattes. You *have* tried one, haven't you?"

"Yes, just this morning, actually." Thorne moved to the counter and began unpacking the bag. "The designs she makes with the milk are fantastic."

I did my best to keep my hands in my lap, and away from my lips. Thorne was a surprisingly good kisser, and I'd been distracted all morning by the memory of our performance in the cider line. Though, that hadn't stopped me from studiously compiling my menu. Now all that was left was to practice making the drinks.

"Kana, this is Thorne. Thorne, meet Kana," I made the introductions.

"It's a pleasure to meet you, Kana." Thorne nodded politely in her direction.

"Oh, no. The pleasure is all mine," she practically purred, her tails swishing excitedly. She lowered her voice to whisper to me, "I like this one much better. When's the wedding? I'll cater it!"

My ears turned pink, and I quietly shot back, "It's not like that, Kana! Did you miss the whole fake relationship explanation?!"

"Does that mean I can date him next?" She gave me a saucy grin, and Thorne turned around abruptly and started coughing.

My face went ever redder. How good was that man's hearing?!

"No!" I said without thinking, before clamping my lips shut. Why had I said that? After the month was up, Thorne was free to see whomever he pleased.

"Uh-huh. He's a keeper, that one. Don't let him get away." Kana took another long sip of her coffee, watching me knowingly over the rim of the cup.

I had half a mind to hex her coffee so that it splashed up in her face. By the way she started chugging it, she could probably tell what I was thinking.

"Anyways, I think I will leave you two to your brewing session for those last couple drinks. After all, if I'm going to be supplying you with my bakery's famous pastries and muffins for your grand opening tomorrow, I had better get to work!" With a wink and a wave, Kana sashayed out the door.

There was silence for a heartbeat, and then Thorne gave a rusty chuckle. "Well, she is quite the character."

"You can say that again." Despite my scowls at Kana earlier, my heart felt lighter after our conversation. Bringing my empty cup over to the sink, I asked Thorne, "Are you ready to try your first pumpkin spice latte?"

"Ready as I'll ever be," he said a tad warily, while rolling up his sleeves.

My eyes tracked the motion, and I noticed how his shadowy tattoos were engraved in a way that incorporated the scars on his arms. I wondered again what he had done for a living before he wandered into Willowmere.

"Don't worry—it's not too different from a mocha. Here, you can help me make it." Picking up a pair of mugs, I moved in front of my precious espresso machine and started it up. "First, you brew the espresso. While I do that, would you bring over the pumpkin puree you got and the jar of cinnamon?"

He did as I asked, moving as silently as the shadows that almost seemed to wisp off of his form. I became acutely aware of his presence at my back as he reached to place both ingredients next me.

"What's next?" He placed one hand on my waist, as if it were the most natural thing in the world to do.

"Next, we mix in the pumpkin—and I like to add a drop of vanilla." I scooped the paste in and stirred it before dropping in the vanilla extract. "Now, it's time to use the wand to heat up some milk."

He watched me as I worked, but once the foam was beginning to form, he surprised me by asking, "Can I try?"

"Sure. Just be careful to keep the wand at this angle so you don't spill any or burn yourself." I carefully handed it over to him, and was pleasantly surprised when he continued using the wand flawlessly. He must have been paying close attention to my demonstration.

"That's a good place to stop–there's just the right amount of foam." I turned it off, before pouring the steaming espresso into two mugs. "Now comes the fun part."

I grabbed a spoon and used it to hold back the foam as I poured the milk into each mug, jiggling the milk pitcher to make a cat-shaped design with the lines in each cup. "Silas insisted that I learn how to make this particular design. Sometimes he gets upset if I don't do a cat design for too long."

It is one of your better designs, after all. Silas sniffed haughtily.

You just like it because it looks like you. I rolled my eyes.

If witches were as cute as cats, you would understand. He settled into his loafing position on top of the cat tree. *Oh, and I want the leftover foam.*

Fine, you can have some—but only if you refrain from pilfering the groceries Thorne just got.

That can be arranged, Silas sniffed.

After carefully scooping the extra foam into a little dish for Silas, I added a bit of foam to each cup, sprinkled some cinnamon on top, and presented one of the mugs to Thorne. He took it carefully, his fingers brushing against mine and lingering for a moment too long.

I took a cautious sip, savoring the rich flavor. Thorne followed my lead, and I laughed when he lowered his cup. A mustache made of foam coated his upper lip, and I couldn't help the giggle that escaped me at the sight.

He pinched his brows together. "What?"

"You have a little foam on your lip."

Thorne licked his lips, but he somehow managed to miss most of it. "Did I get it?"

"Not quite." I set my cup down and leaned forward, using my thumb to wipe away the foam. His lip was soft under my finger, and without thinking, I licked my finger clean.

Thorne's violet eyes deepened into pools of the darkest amethyst. He deliberately took another sip, replacing all the foam I had just wiped off.

"I'm not the only one, you know. Let me get that for you." He set his own mug down and brought his hand to my face, but instead of tracing my lips, he leaned closer and kissed me.

The first time he had kissed me was magical. This time, it was divine.

He tasted like pumpkin spice, his lips soft and searching on mine. Warm cinnamon filled my nostrils, and I breathed it in like a drowning woman in search of air.

This was only meant to be a pretend relationship. But could I deny that I was beginning to wish it wasn't?

Almost as if he sensed the direction of my thoughts, Thorne's thumb stroked my cheek so tenderly that I wanted to melt. How was it possible that being with Thorne felt so right? It was easy and comfortable in a way I had never before experienced.

And then Rasmus burst through the door.

I really needed to remember to lock that thing.

Why didn't you warn me? I knew Silas would have heard him coming.

I couldn't hear him over the sound of you two licking each other's faces. He flicked his tail irritably. *Besides, I like seeing that fishy look on his face when he sees you with the Dark One.*

Rasmus did indeed look like a fish out of water. His mouth hung open as he took in the scene Thorne and I must have made. A vein throbbed in his forehead, and his face grew progressively closer to matching the color of his ginger hair.

"Don't you ever knock?!" As soon as the words left my lips, I grimaced. I was one to talk, considering how I had walked in on Thorne.

And by the look in Thorne's eyes when he glanced at me, one scarred eyebrow raised, he was thinking the same thing.

"Clover! What the hell are you doing, acting like such a tramp?!" He strode forward angrily, until he was on the other side of the counter. "Because of you, I'm the laughingstock of this whole backwater town! And don't even get me started on that little stunt you pulled in front of my parents last night—at this rate, I'll never hear the end of it!"

"Leave, warlock. You have no business here," Thorne warned him, stepping in front of me protectively.

But Rasmus' shoulders were heaving with emotion. He glared at me, before his gaze switched to Thorne. "And I've heard all about *you,* you rotten shadowmancer. Someone who would abandon his entire party to die in a dungeon has no business leeching off of—"

Shadows erupted from the ground and wrapped around Rasmus' throat, cutting off his air and his incessant tirade. All emotion had drained from Thorne's face, and he stood as still and stiff as a statue carved from onyx. Darkness poured off of him like smoke, but it was the ice in his expression that sent a chill down my spine.

Had Thorne really done something like that? Sure, I didn't know much about the man, but from what I had seen so far, he didn't seem like the type of person who would do such a thing.

Thorne walked slowly and deliberately towards Rasmus as the potion master slowly levitated off the ground, his feet dangling helplessly. It became suddenly, abundantly clear to me that Thorne had fought a warlock before; he knew that a witch or warlock who could not speak, could not cast spells or hexes.

"Fools who have never faced death and paid his price should keep their traps shut, and mind their own damn business." The shadowmancer's voice was lethally quiet, like feathers made of steel.

Rasmus' eyes bulged as he clawed uselessly at his neck. But shadows have no substance, so his scrabbling hands passed easily through them.

"Thorne...?" I asked quietly when the warlock's eyes began to roll back in his head. Surely, he wouldn't actually kill my ex...right? I hated Rasmus, but I didn't exactly want him dead.

Thorne flinched, glancing back at me with an unreadable expression on his face. Immediately, the shadows dispersed, and Rasmus fell to the floor in a heap, coughing violently. The hands he brought to his throat shook.

"Get out." Thorne didn't raise his voice, but Rasmus scrambled to his feet and bolted out the door like he had seen a ghost, his face as white as a sheet.

Without looking at me, Thorne pulled on his coat and headed for the door.

"Thorne, wait! Where are you going?"

"I'm not going after him, if that's what you're worried about. The ruddy bastard will keep breathing just fine until he pisses off the wrong person again." His voice was like gravel, and he still wouldn't look at me.

"That's not what I meant." I slowly walked towards Thorne when he hesitated, his hand on the doorknob.

"Then what *did* you mean?"

"Why are you leaving? You haven't even finished your latte yet." I knew it was a flimsy excuse.

But he still turned around. "You...don't want me to go?"

"Of course not!" I said with feeling, walking over until I stood right in front of him.

"You're not...afraid of me?" Thorne's cold demeanor cracked, his eyes finally finding mine. "After what I just did?"

I leaned up on my toes, bracing my hands against his chest. "No."

"You should be." His voice was like gravel.

"Says who?" I whispered.

"Me."

I tilted my chin up, bringing our faces inches apart. "Are you going to hurt *me*, Thorne?"

"Never." He said the word like a solemn vow.

"Then I have no reason to be afraid."

"Even if what that warlock said were true?" he breathed, fear and hope chasing each other through the depths of his eyes.

I placed a hand on his face. "I may not have known you long, Thorne, but I know you well enough to tell that's not something you would do. I have a feeling there's much more to the story than that. And if you want to talk about it, I'm here to listen."

Thorne leaned into my touch, closing his eyes. The late afternoon light gilded the side of his face, softening his expression. And when he finally opened his violet eyes, there was an openness there that left me breathless.

"I think I might just take you up on your offer." He searched my eyes, looking for any sign that I hadn't truly meant what I'd said. When he found none, he placed his hand over my smaller one. "Would you...like to stay for dinner?"

"Absolutely."

Chapter Nine

Spells & Stories

Clove

"I promise I'm a much better cook than barista," Thorne said almost sheepishly, as he held his apartment door open for me later that evening.

"Oh? Then it sounds like I am in for quite the treat." Since I had cooked for both myself and Rasmus, I also knew my way around a kitchen. However, it felt nice to not be expected to do all of the cooking. "Is there anything I can do to help?"

He thought about it for a moment as we entered the kitchen. "Would you make the salad while I work on the stew?"

"Sure thing," I said with a smile.

But after I finished washing my hands, I turned around to see that Thorne had donned a frilly pink apron covered in little cat illustrations. I started giggling, then slapped a hand over my mouth to try and contain the sound, but it was too late.

Thorne's ears turned an adorable shade of pink that nearly matched the apron. "Mrs. Virgil left it behind," he explained a tad stiffly, then held up a nearly identical apron, but in purple. "Fortunately, she kept extras."

"How very practical of her." I grinned as I put the apron on, and tied the sash into a little bow at the back. "She has marvelous taste; I'm sure Silas would approve."

"I've no doubt," he said drily.

Thorne moved to the fridge and pulled out a bag of fresh lettuce, shredded carrots, and several dressing options, and plopped them in front of me. He then used his shadows to pull out a cutting board, a large pot, and a multitude of ingredients for beef stew.

"Where did you learn to cook?" I asked, as we both set about preparing our ingredients.

Thorne grimaced, but his tone was light as he replied, "I've had to spend a lot of time traveling with groups of men—mercenaries, adventurers, and the like. Most of them couldn't tell the difference between an onion and an apple, and I got tired fairly quickly of subsisting off of cold jerky and hardtack."

I shuddered. "I can imagine, but I certainly don't want to."

The shadowmancer scraped his chopped vegetables into the simmering broth. "My first few attempts at cooking were fairly disastrous; my omelets had egg shells in them, and my stews were chock-full of salt and way too much garlic. It took me longer than I care to admit to figure out that when a recipe called for a clove of garlic, it didn't mean the entire bulb."

"Yikes! I hope everyone else in your party liked garlic." I laughed as I ripped the lettuce into bite-size pieces. "Don't feel too bad. My first few potions blew up in my face—literally!"

Thorne paused to glance over at me with concern. "They did? Were you hurt?"

"My pride took the biggest hit. Though it took my eyebrows a couple months to grow back." I grinned at the memory.

"An eyebrow-less Clove? Now that I have to see." He returned to slicing up the meat.

"I'm sure my mom has pictures somewhere," I admitted, laughing a little self-consciously. "Probably in a scrapbook spelled against fire, lightning, and water."

"Lightning?" He raised an eyebrow in my direction, and added the meat to the pot. He capped it with a lid to let it simmer.

I blushed. "Every witch goes through a lightning phase in high school. I tried to burn that embarrassing photo with a lightning strike before anyone could see it. Dramatic, I know." I rolled my eyes at my past self.

"I would have simply put it down the garbage disposal in the sink."

I blinked at him. "That's brilliant! Why didn't I ever think of that?!"

Thorne shrugged. "I've noticed the magically-inclined tend to overthink these things. Simple is usually best."

"You make a good point. But why do things with your hands when you can have them done for you?" I flicked my wrist, and watched with a satisfied smile as the carrot slices floated into the salad bowl and a balsamic vinaigrette poured itself on top. With a twirl of my finger, the salad mixed itself to perfection.

"Not bad. But can you cook the stew perfectly without burning it?" There was a light of challenge in his eyes that I had no intention of backing down from.

"Of course! I never use the microwave." I flicked my long hair over my shoulder and held out a hand towards the pot. My hand and the pot glowed purple as I concentrated on speeding up the cooking process, while still maintaining the appropriate temperature. Once its savory smell filled the air, I released the spell.

Time acceleration magic was fairly advanced, but I had been determined to master it. After all, microwaved food just didn't taste nearly as good.

"Your magic is beautiful. Unlike mine," he murmured, almost so quietly that I missed it.

"Your darkness is beautiful, too. Like the shade beneath an oak tree in the summer, and a sky full of stars in the spring." I brushed my hand through a wispy shadow, watching as it swirled and eddied like smoke in the breeze.

A tendril of darkness wrapped gently around my wrist for a moment, conveying silent thanks. Thorne was looking at me like I was a puzzle, one he couldn't quite solve.

"I'm sure you will find the stew is cooked to perfection," I said to break the silence. "I'll set the table while you dish it up."

Thorne blinked, as if coming out of a trance, and nodded. "Of course."

I went ahead and set out the napkins and utensils, listening as the quiet clinking of plates filled the air. Conjuring a few candles, I set them on the table and lit them with lively orange flames. A pair of shadowy tendrils deposited two glasses of sparkling water on the table, and a moment later, Thorne arrived, carrying the food.

I reached to pull out a chair, but one of Thorne's shadows beat me to it. "Why, what a gentleman. Thank you," I told the shadow as I sat down and it scooted my chair in.

What sounded suspiciously like a concealed laugh came from the other side of the table, but when I looked, Thorne was already taking a sip of his stew. "Cooked to perfection," he said approvingly.

I grinned. "I told you it would be." I took a sip as well, savoring the rich flavor of the broth. Thorne had done an excellent job seasoning it. "If you're this good at seasoning food, I have no doubt you will become a master barista in no time."

"I'm glad you like it." A small smile graced his lips. "I've found that a warm meal with the right spices can do wonders for the mood."

"I have a feeling that just your cooking alone would have made you a valuable member of any expedition."

"You would think." His smile dimmed, and I kicked myself for bringing it up first; I didn't want to force him to share his story with me. But when he remained silent, I decided that he might have an easier time opening up to me if I shared a little about myself first.

"I suppose I owe you an explanation," I started, pushing my salad around my plate with my fork. I tried not to let my mood sink too low as my thoughts returned to the memories I had been working so hard to bury.

He frowned. "For what?"

"For what happened between me and Rasmus. Why, when he showed up, I felt the need to pretend I had a boyfriend." I took a deep breath, determined to keep my voice steady.

Thorne reached across the table to place his hand over mine. "You don't owe me anything, Clove. If you're not ready..."

I shook my head. "I think talking about things like this helps release some of the hurt that's been festering."

Thorne's eyes took on a melancholy cast; he understood I wasn't just talking about myself. But he nodded all the same, his thumb moving in soothing circles on my wrist.

"I met Rasmus in college. We were the only two spellcasters in our year, so we hit it off. He was considerate back then, and I loved listening to him talk about his hopes and dreams for the future. We had so much fun coming up with new spells and potions together, in between our mundane literature and history classes," I began wistfully. "We both graduated with our master's degrees, and moved in together while we began our careers in Seattle."

Thorne nodded, silently encouraging me to continue.

"But he's from an old, affluent family, and I knew he felt immense pressure from them to be successful, and to take over the family business one day. I knew his parents never really approved of me, and I could guess it was because I wasn't from one of the more prestigious covens. His mother in particular kept trying to set him up with Nyssa, a witch from *her* coven, who had the 'proper' pedigree." My voice started to shake as I got to the part of the story that had been featuring in my nightmares lately.

"Unfortunately, that sort of thinking is all too common in many magical communities," Thorne commented softly. "That's what makes Willowmere so special."

"Exactly. And Rasmus always assured me that they'd come around eventually. So when he proposed, I thought we had left all that behind us, that his parents had finally given us their blessing. I foolishly believed him—until I came home early from the office one day, to find Rasmus and Nyssa in our bed together."

"So that's why you came back to Willowmere." There was no pity in his violet eyes; just sympathy and heartache.

"I was so angry that I threw the ring at him, hexed his underwear drawer, and stormed out with just Silas and a few of my things." My voice wobbled, and I felt tears pricking my eyes.

"You hexed his underwear drawer?" Thorne sounded impressed, rather than judgmental. "With what?"

"I hexed it to insult the size of his...wand every time he opened it." I laughed shakily.

Thorne's shoulders shook with silent laughter. "Well done. Is that why he seems so angry all the time?"

I scowled. "I cannot fathom why *he's* angry. *I'm* the one who has that right, after he betrayed me like that. Or why he continues to pester me."

"Hmm. Based on our little interaction with Bellatrix, I would guess that he intended to break up with you officially, *before* publicly dating the other witch—to preserve his reputation." Thorne scoffed. "Once that was no longer an option, I bet he wanted to frame *you* as the one who cheated."

"That...actually makes perfect sense," I mused. Everything fit. "Though I still can't believe I never noticed this side of him until it was nearly too late."

"People change," Thorne said sadly. "And not always for the better. Just know that Rasmus' decisions were not your fault."

I gave him a watery smile. "Thank you."

Thorne looked to be deep in thought as we finished our meal, but my heart felt much lighter. When we were done, he cleared away our plates, but before he could wash them, I offered, "Allow me."

Purple magic glimmered in the air as I had the dishes wash and dry themselves and return to their places in the cabinet.

Thorne whistled. "Now *that* is a neat trick."

"One of my favorites—and most-used. Would you like some coffee with dessert?" I had picked up some celebratory cheesecake earlier this afternoon, in anticipation of officially opening my coffee shop. But it seemed we had something else to celebrate now: the sharing of our stories.

"That would be great. I'll pull the cheesecake out of the fridge." He gave me a small smile.

"Then I will be right back." It took me only a few minutes to pop down to the shop and make a pair of mochas—with extra chocolate and cream. While I did, I heard it start raining, the sound of raindrops pattering on the windows a very pleasant one.

More coffee? Silas asked from his perch. *Are you not planning to sleep tonight?*

Nope. I'm much too nervous for that, I quipped back. *Besides, I'll have to be up early for the grand opening tomorrow anyways.*

By the time I came back, Thorne had moved the candles to the coffee table in front of the small sofa—which had a nice view out the window of the rainy night.

"Here you go," I said as I handed him a steaming mug and sat down beside him on the sofa.

"Thank you." He set a slice of cheesecake in front of me, and I wasted no time digging in. "I...wanted to apologize for losing my temper earlier, with Rasmus. I didn't want you to see me like that."

He looked over at me all solemnly, but started chuckling when he saw my cheesecake-stuffed cheeks. "I guess I don't have to wonder what a chipmunk would look like if it had a taste for cheesecake."

I blushed, and swallowed down my treat. "I have a sweet tooth, alright?"

"Duly noted." His smile set butterflies loose in my stomach, but I tried to push them down.

"There's no need to apologize," I said gently. "Honestly, if you hadn't shut him up, I would have."

Thorne ran a hand through his dark hair, and my fingers itched to do the same. I wrapped them around my warm mug instead. I was becoming far too attached.

This was only temporary, after all. I needed to remember that.

"I would have liked to see that," he said almost ruefully. He took a sip of his mocha—which was more milk than coffee at this point—and began in a halting voice, "Shadowmancers have always been rare. But rarer still are shadowmancers with the power to create shadow soldiers—and they are always used as tools of war."

I took another sip to disguise my gasp of surprise. I had only ever heard legends of shadowmancers *that* powerful in the age of myth, before the magical races went into hiding.

Thorne grimaced, gazing down into his coffee with haunted eyes. "My parents were thrilled. From the age of eight, I was trained to be a living weapon. I excelled. When I was ten, I went on my first raid. By the time I was twelve, I was out on campaigns more than I was home, and I was bringing in more income than both of my parents combined. And by the time I turned twenty, I couldn't take it anymore."

I rested a hand on his shoulder, grieving for a little boy whose childhood had been stolen from him.

"So I disappeared. I created a new identity and everything, and got as far away from my parents as I could. I swore I would never summon my soldiers for someone else's meaningless war ever again. Once I arrived on the west coast, I took up adventuring—something I had always wanted to try." His laugh was humorless.

"But because I kept most of my abilities hidden, few parties would hire me. So, when one finally did, I was thrilled. I worked for them for a few months, and I loved exploring the dungeons. Finding hidden treasures and vanquishing monsters was just as amazing as I'd hoped it would be."

I nodded silently. I had never been in a dungeon myself, but I had certainly enjoyed listening to the stories of those who had.

"But one day, my party triggered a trap unlike anything we had encountered before. Opening a treasure chest summoned a horde of monsters, and the exit door began to close. Just as I was about to summon my soldiers to protect us, the warlock in my party cast a paralysis hex on me. They used me as bait for the monsters so that they could escape."

My hand flew to my mouth in horror. No wonder Thorne seemed to hold such animosity for warlocks.

Thorne took a deep, shuddering breath. "But I don't need to move to summon my shadows; they respond to my will. They took down the monsters with ease. But by the time the hex wore off and I found the hidden exit, the rest of the party were nowhere to be found. I escaped that dungeon alone, assuming they had left long before me. But according to the guild, none of them ever returned."

By this point, I was absolutely steaming mad. "And they blamed *you* for your party members' deaths?! After the way *they* sacrificed *you?!*"

Thorne looked at me with haunted eyes. "They didn't believe me. And there's no way to prove a negative, to prove something I *didn't* do."

I set my cup aside, and gently put Thorne's on the coffee table as well. I drew him into a hug, stroking his back soothingly.

"Is that why you came to Willowmere? Why some of the elders refused to rent to you?"

He went stiff in my arms, but gradually relaxed. His arms slowly encircled me, and he rested his head on my shoulder. "Yes," he whispered.

After a minute, Thorne pulled back. But when he remained silent, I took his face in my hands, forcing him to meet my eyes. He looked startled, but made no move to pull away again.

"If what Rasmus did wasn't my fault, then what that party did to you wasn't your fault, either." I surprised even myself with the force of my words.

"But, my powers...if I'd only told them the truth..." Guilt laced his voice, his eyes.

"If it hadn't been *you,* that party would have betrayed someone else. And that someone else would not have made it back." There was no doubt in my tone. "Even if you *had* told them the truth, it sounds like they would have tried to use you the same way your parents did."

"I know that in my head," he whispered, his eyes turning glassy. "But..."

"But it still hurts," I finished. "It still makes you wonder if somehow, you're the problem. If you're broken."

He swallowed. Nodded.

It seemed both of us were trying to pick up the pieces of our lives. It made me feel a little better to know that I wasn't the only one feeling this way.

"Maybe we can be broken together, and slowly pick up the pieces. We can glue them back together with gold instead of tears, until we're stronger than we were before." I laced my fingers through his and squeezed.

"I used to think I was just unlucky with people. Unlucky with my party, unlucky with my parents… But now, I think…maybe I just hadn't met the right person yet." His voice dropped an octave, and he lifted my hand to his lips.

My heart melted. It was in that moment, with startling clarity, that I realised I was falling in love with him, shadows, scars, and all.

CHAPTER TEN

Tea & Trouble

CLOVE

"**T**his is it." I stood facing the closed front door, trying to mentally prepare myself to flip the CLOSED sign to OPEN.

You can always open tomorrow, complained Silas, cracking one eye open. *And go back to bed for today.*

You know I can't do that—I told everyone I was opening today, *not tomorrow.* I tried unsuccessfully to cover my yawn. I had been far too excited to sleep.

At least let me *sleep, then,* he grumbled, curling up in his little house.

Today was the grand opening of The Broom & Bean, the day I had been dreaming of for so long. But even though I was incredibly excited, I was also incredibly nervous. What if something went wrong? Or worse, what if Rasmus barged in again and tried to humiliate me in front of everyone?

But at least I wouldn't be doing this alone.

"No matter how today goes, I'm proud of you." Thorne placed a hand on my shoulder. After last night's openness, it felt like we had grown much closer. "And I can tell your parents are proud of you, too."

I furrowed my brow. "You've met my parents?"

"No, but I think I'm about to." He chuckled, gesturing at the window through which, sure enough, I could see my parents waiting eagerly.

I laughed, flipping the sign so that it read OPEN, and propped open the door. The little bell I had installed tinkled merrily as my mom greeted me with a hug, and my dad greeted Thorne with a firm handshake.

"Thank you for coming!" It meant more to me than they knew to have their support, despite my recent and rather drastic change in life plans.

"How could we possibly miss it?" my mom asked with a warm smile, which quickly turned mischievous. "Though, we're not the only ones."

"What?" I peered around my parents, my confusion quickly turning into delight when I spotted the line of people behind them.

"Well?" Thorne prompted gently. "Your customers are waiting!"

That jolted me into action. I announced, "Thank you for your support, everyone! The Broom & Bean is now officially open; please, come on in!"

I moved behind the counter as the line of people shuffled inside. Thorne settled into a seat with the mocha I had made him earlier this morning and ate his breakfast pastry. He had kindly offered to man the till whenever I needed to take a break.

"What can I get for my very first customers?" I grinned at my mom and dad.

"Oh, how about a pair of medium mochas and two of those croissants in the case?" my dad said, pulling out his wallet.

"Coming right up!" I put the croissants in the toaster oven to warm up while I went about making the mochas. Thanks to my magic, I was able to have both drinks made by the time the croissants were warm. "Here you go."

"Thank you, pumpkin." My dad plopped a tip in the tip jar as he grabbed his order, and they both settled into a cozy corner table near Silas' cat tree to enjoy it.

"Next please," I called.

Kana practically skipped up to the till, her fox tails swishing behind her. "Congratulations on opening! I love how cozy you made the café."

"Thank you for coming, Kana—and for your delicious croissants. I have a feeling they'll soon be one of our best sellers!" I gave her a little wink.

"Naturally. Though I bet sales will go through the roof when I bring over some of my famous pumpkin muffins." She grinned like a fox in a henhouse. "I've been dying to try one of your pumpkin spice lattes."

"Sure thing!" I made sure to sprinkle an extra-generous helping of cinnamon on top, just the way she liked it.

"Thank you," she said as I handed her cup over. "I have to get back to the bakery, but I'm sure today will go magnificently for you."

My next customer was one of the waitresses I had seen working at the diner down the street. She was taller than me, with pointed ears and gently curved horns emerging from her fiery red hair. Her almond-shaped eyes were a reddish-gold that glowed like lava. If I remembered correctly, she and her family of firedrake shifters had moved to Willowmere only a year or two before I left for college, so I had only really seen her in passing.

"Hi, I don't believe we've met. I'm Mei, of the Flameborn Fleet." She fingered her horns self-consciously.

"It's nice to officially meet you, Mei! I'm Clove—of the Morelli Coven." I smiled reassuringly at her. "I've tried the dumplings at your diner—they're better than anything I've had in Seattle."

Mei beamed at me. "My parents will be thrilled to hear that." She lowered her voice conspiratorially. "Though between you and me, our coffee is nothing special. So I'm excited to try your GlimmerBrew."

I laughed. "Duly noted—thanks for the warning. I hope you like my GlimmerBrew—it changes colors and sometimes flavors with every sip."

Mei's eyes brightened as she pulled out her wallet. "That sounds loads more interesting than anything the regular, mainstream coffee franchises can whip up."

"Much more flavorful—and with a hint of magic." I winked at her, and quickly made her drink while she paid. "Here you go. I hope you enjoy it! I'll be sure to stop by the diner soon."

After Mei left, I had a steady stream of customers. Mei's parents stopped by, and so did a couple of Kana's employees. I saw a few old friends and neighbors, and got to meet several of the other shop owners on main street. Mermaids, elves, vampires and fae walked through my door, and even an orc and a werewolf stopped by.

Even Mr. Chevalier, the centaur real estate agent, came to purchase some coffee. Though when he spotted Thorne watching him from the corner, his long ears started to twitch nervously.

Needless to say, I did *not* give him the friends and family discount. And thanks to Thorne's presence, he didn't dare complain.

Though I supposed I wasn't exactly upset about my surprise tenant. At least, not anymore.

I took a little break to have lunch with my parents. From our conversation, I could tell that they had been more worried about my decision to buy the shop than they'd let on. But after coming to the grand opening, it seemed like some of those fears had been put to rest.

I made sure to continuously check on Thorne, who was manning the counter for me while I ate. Even though his tone with customers had been a bit reserved and clipped to begin with, he had warmed up considerably. I think having a predetermined script, and knowing that the people he was interacting with wanted nothing from him except a beverage or a pastry, helped immensely.

Two days ago, I would have assumed he was simply bad with people. But after he had shared his story with me last night, I now knew he was simply wary of them—even if that wariness seemed standoffish from the outside looking in.

Though I did catch a few of the ladies sending him admiring glances when he wasn't looking. He looked good in my branded purple apron; the color matched his eyes. Thorne's handsome face might actually bring in more business than my magical drinks if I got him to help out more often.

If I offered him a job working in my little coffee shop, would he take it? Could that entice him to stay in Willowmere? Did I want him to?

"It looks like you two have been getting along well these days," my mother said with a knowing look, when she caught me glancing over at Thorne once again.

I blushed, but instead of denying it, I simply said, "We have."

My mom exchanged a look with my dad.

"We're glad to see you so happy, Clove. It's been far too long since we saw you so relaxed and at peace." He placed his hand over my mother's and gave it a pat.

"You're not...disappointed in me?" I whispered around the sudden lump in my throat. This path was the exact opposite of the one they had encouraged me to take all my life. "For opening a shop instead of climbing the corporate ladder?"

"We could never be disappointed in you." My mother took my hands and gave them a squeeze. "We realize now that...we were so focused on making sure you had all of the opportunities we never did, that we never stopped to ask you what it was that *you* wanted."

I raised my eyes to hers, to find that they were lined with tears. "Do you mean it?"

My dad put his hand on my shoulder. "Absolutely, pumpkin. We want what's best for you—whatever that entails."

"That means more than you know." I gave them a watery smile.

I told you they'd come around eventually. Silas hopped into my dad's lap and butted his hand affectionately, so that the older warlock would scratch him under the chin just the way he liked it.

After a few minutes, my dad then cleared his throat. "Well, your mom and I should head home—we still have a few potion orders left to fill."

"I'll make your favorite for dinner—spaghetti bolognese." She pulled me into a quick hug before she and dad headed out.

It was with a much lighter heart that I walked into the back room and donned my purple apron. I tied my hair up into a high ponytail, feeling like I was on top of the world. I knew not every day would be as busy as today, but with the support of the community, I had a feeling everything was going to be just fine.

Or at least I did, until I emerged from the back room to see my ex-fiance's mistress standing at the counter, and flirting with *my* shadowmancer.

I hadn't exactly gotten a good look at her the last time I saw her. I hated to admit that she was pretty, at least by classic witch standards. Nyssa had a good two inches on me, and her dark green hair was styled in a perfect bob. Dark kohl lined her black eyes, and a string of earrings marched up each ear. Bangles clattered at her wrists and rings crowded her manicured fingers. Even her short little dress screamed *designer.* But I supposed I should have expected as much from a witch of the powerful Maeve Coven.

I scanned the room, and spotted Rasmus seated at one of the corner tables, looking like he would rather be anywhere else. I noted with some satisfaction that he was deliberately avoiding looking in Thorne's direction.

Plastering on my best customer service smile, I stalked over until I stood right next to Thorne.

"There you are, Clove! Your employee here was refusing to go and get you," Nyssa said haughtily, as if all service workers were beneath her.

It appeared Rasmus hadn't told her about his little run-in with Thorne and his shadows yesterday. If only she knew what the man she'd just insulted was capable of.

"My employee," I drawled, placing one hand on his bicep possessively, "knows better than to interrupt me on my break." I looked her up and down scathingly, pushing down my lingering hurt. "What was it that you needed to talk about so desperately with me?"

Nyssa scowled, her eyes lingering on the hand touching Thorne. "I came to warn you."

Thorne stiffened beneath my hand.

But I simply raised an eyebrow at the other witch. "About what?"

"To stay away from Rasmus. He's mine," she practically growled.

I laughed. "You can have him."

She blinked, clearly taken aback. "What?"

"You deserve each other, and as you can see, I am happily taken." I wound my arm around Thorne's, leaning into him. "I actually have a favor to ask of you, Nyssa."

"You do?" The witch looked cautiously optimistic.

"Yes. You see, I am trying to go my separate way from the two of you, but for some reason, Rasmus keeps seeking me out." I sighed dramatically, glancing pointedly in Rasmus' direction. "Would you be so kind as to keep him away from me?"

"Gladly." Nyssa snorted, but then gave me the side-eye. "But...aren't you upset? I know you were the one who hexed his dresser drawer."

I paused, and felt Thorne look down at me, silently asking if he should intervene. I gave his arm a squeeze. "Not anymore. Another witch would want revenge; I just want to be left alone with my cozy shop, my little espresso machine, and...my new boyfriend."

I almost surprised myself, but I knew I spoke the truth. I had thought about taking revenge at first; but then I would have been stewing in my hatred and resentment, and the only person that would have hurt was *me*.

Thorne put his arm around me, pressing a light kiss to my cheek. Rasmus must have been watching us after all, because he suddenly rose from his self-imposed exile and stormed to the front of the now-growing line.

"With garbage like this on the menu, it'll be a wonder if this place lasts longer than a week," he sneered, holding his coffee up for emphasis.

All the conversations in the shop died a quick death. Every pair of eyes turned to the redheaded warlock, who started fidgeting uncomfortably. Nyssa looked mortified.

Had this cheater *really* decided to try and ruin my lifelong dream, my precious fledgling business that I'd poured my heart and soul into, because he was jealous Thorne had kissed me on the cheek? After *he* had cheated on *me?*

"It's probably made with cheap beans," he stammered into the silence. "The color-changing spell is juvenile, and only a real potions master like me could—"

A particularly muscular werewolf and orc abruptly stood up and faced Rasmus, who looked like he was about ready to wet himself—or fire off some ill-advised spells.

But before a fight could break out, Thorne vaulted smoothly over the counter, so that he towered over Rasmus. Wisps of shadow poured from his frame, pooling at his feet like a dark fog.

"Now hold on..." Rasmus swallowed nervously and backed up a step into his mistress, trying to avoid touching them. "I was only saying what everyone was thinking."

"That's funny," I finally chimed in, after overcoming my initial shock. "I seem to remember you drank this particular brew down by the gallon practically every morning—and would giggle like a schoolgirl when it changed color. You didn't seem to have a problem with it then."

"Seriously?" Nyssa was now scowling at Rasmus instead of me.

"That's not— I can explain!" His eyes glanced wildly around the room, but he was met only with cold stares.

"If you're not going to order anything else, I am going to have to ask you to leave—along with your *mistress.*" Thorne's tone was nearly as deep and dark as his shadows.

Whispers and murmurs broke out. Nyssa and Rasmus both reddened, and she began tugging on his arm to usher him out.

"Fine! I wouldn't want to waste a single one of my hard-earned dollars on this bean water anyway," Rasmus spat, as he finally allowed Nyssa to lead him out.

"Don't you mean your *father's* hard-earned dollars?" I called after him.

To her credit, Nyssa managed to get him under control before he could retort and dig himself a deeper hole.

A few titters and chuckles echoed around the room, lightening the atmosphere. The orc and the werewolf sat back down, and it felt like a collective sigh of relief was released.

"Thanks." I gave Thorne a tight smile as he returned to stand beside me—by walking around the counter like a normal person this time.

"Anytime." His comforting presence made me feel like I could finally relax.

The person who had been waiting in line behind Nyssa, an older selkie and her granddaughter, finally stepped forward to place her order, which I made as speedily as I could manage. I handed over the croissant she ordered for her granddaughter, and she gave me a warm smile.

"You look like you could use a cup of tea, dearie," she said, patting my arm comfortingly.

I sighed, rubbing my temples. "I think I've had about as much *tea* as I can handle for one day. Or lifetime."

The older woman looked confused, until her little granddaughter tugged on her sleeve and whispered in her ear, "She means too much gossip and drama."

"Slang these days," the grandmother tutted. "Confuses us poor old folks to no end."

"You don't look a day over thirty-five, madam," Thorne said suavely.

"Young'uns these days." She waved him off, but looked quite pleased as she took her coffee and croissant over to an open seat by the crackling hearth, where her granddaughter promptly curled up happily with her treat.

"Sorry for the interruption everyone, and thanks for standing up for me. Free refills are on the house!" I announced.

A collective cheer went up, and I smiled to myself. Losing a bit of money on my opening day seemed like a small price to pay for the scene I had just witnessed, and for the warmth that filled this room. My customers had given me more than just help or protection; they had given me new hope, and the sense of community I had been yearning for, but didn't know I needed.

CHAPTER ELEVEN

Cats & Carvings

THORNE

Anything to report? I asked my soldiers.

Negative, stated the one outside Clove's house.

Nothing, answered the one stationed at the shop.

Nothing relevant, answered the soldier I had placed in Rasmus' shadow, after his little outburst during the shop's grand opening. *The warlock has been spending the bulk of his time arguing with his mistress, being scolded by his parents, or yelling at his computer.*

I see. Continue your observations, and report back to me if anything changes.

Yes, my lord, they replied in unison.

I sighed, pinching the bridge of my nose. I preferred eliminating threats immediately. Monitoring them was exhausting, and I wasn't even the one doing most of the watching!

But at least this way, I could keep Clove safe. So far, Rasmus hadn't made any other stupid moves, and I hoped he would keep it that way. Though I was still surprised the warlock hadn't noticed the shadow soldier I had slipped into his shadow. His parents must have sheltered him a great deal for him to be so completely oblivious.

Then again, maybe *I* was the strange one. I had to keep reminding myself that most people, magical or otherwise, did not have nearly as much experience in battle as I did.

At least that experience allowed me to protect Clove now. Even if it made me feel like a shark in a pond full of guppies.

I returned my gaze to Clove. At the moment, she was helping what was likely her last customer for the night. Leaning back in the stuffed armchair I had claimed as my own, I watched the way her smile warmed up the entire room, far more than the crackling fire to my right. She used her magic so effortlessly, as if it were an extension of her being. I had encountered very few witches or warlocks with an equal level of dedication to their craft. Though it seemed she had devoted an equal effort to her brewing skills for both coffee and potions.

The little bell over the door jingled as the customer left, with a cup of steaming GlimmerBrew in hand. Another heartbeat later, and Clove flicked her wrist to magically flip the OPEN sign to CLOSED and locked the door.

Putting her hands on her hips, she exclaimed, "Well, I think I'll call it a day."

"I'm glad business has been going so well this week." I stood, stretching after sitting for so long.

"Me, too." She gave me a relieved smile. "I hope it keeps up."

"I'm sure it will." I walked over to the counter and leaned against it. "By the way, when did you want to carve those pumpkins? I'm assuming you want to have them ready before the Moonlit Masquerade Ball in a few days."

"That's right! I completely forgot about them." Clove tapped her chin thoughtfully. "Why don't we carve them tonight? I can cast a preservation spell on them so they'll last through all the festivities."

I loved the way she said *we*.

"Let's do it."

With a grin, Clove floated two pumpkins over to one of the shop's tables, not too far from the fire and Silas' cat tree. I grabbed a few knives and some spare newspapers.

"What are the newspapers for?" Clove asked as she pulled her hair back into a ponytail.

"For the pulp. That way you don't have more cleaning up to do."

"Good thinking." She sat down and drew one of the pumpkins towards her. Pulling out a marker, she began drawing on her pumpkin.

"What are you drawing?" I asked, edging closer so I could see.

"No peeking!" Clove summoned a curtain of sparkles to hide it. "It's a surprise."

"Fine, fine," I grumbled. "Then you'll have to wait and see what design I go for, too."

"We'll have a grand reveal when we're done." Clove summoned a second marker and floated it over to me.

"Thanks." I sat down as well, but ended up just staring at my pumpkin.

The precious few times I had carved a pumpkin when I was little, I had gone for the classic Jack o'Lantern faces. And usually the mean and scary-looking ones, at that. But somehow, I couldn't picture one of those fitting well in The Broom & Bean.

Stroking my goatee, I tried to come up with something different. Something that wouldn't be out of place in a witch's magical coffee shop. An idea sparked, and I pulled the cap off my pen and got to work.

After a few minutes, I had the basic design sketched out. I had a feeling it wouldn't hold a candle to Clove's, but for once, this wasn't a competition. I picked up one of the larger knives and began cutting a circle around the stem.

"Don't forget to cut at an angle, so the top doesn't fall straight through the hole," Clove advised, watching me with a mildly concerned look on her face.

"I completely forgot." I ran a hand through my hair self-consciously. "It's been a while since the last time I carved one of these."

Clove's expression softened. "Tell me about the last time you carved a pumpkin."

I smiled ruefully. "I think it was when I was seven, before my powers fully manifested. My parents and I used to carve pumpkins every year to decorate for the trick-or-treaters."

"What kinds of designs did you do?" Clove kept her eyes on her own pumpkin, but her tone was warm and open.

"Mostly the typical scary Jack o'Lantern faces. They weren't very good, but it was fun making them. How about you?"

"Pretty much the same. Though in recent years, I've started tackling some of the more complicated patterns, like howling wolves and haunted houses." She smiled to herself. "Isn't it funny how the legends of magic and the people who wielded it have continued on amongst humans?"

"Very." But then a thought occurred to me. "Don't you find it insulting how humans always depict witches as old hags with green skin or beaky noses?"

"Not really—I don't take it personally." She shook her head. "I bet there were plenty of elder witches terrorizing the humans who *did* look like that. Besides, they have plenty of cute witches in movies, too."

"They do?" I asked as I set my pumpkin top aside and began scooping out the pulp.

"You haven't seen any of those?" Clove began hollowing out her pumpkin as well.

"Until recently, I didn't have the time or the interest. And before you bought the building, I mostly used candles for light, since there was no electricity or wifi," I explained. Fortunately for me, the water had still worked since it was drawn straight from a well in the basement.

"Right." Clove's cheeks colored a bit in embarrassment.

"Do you have some you recommend?"

Clove's beautiful turquoise eyes lit up. "Oh boy, do I! How much time do you have?"

"All the time in the world." My voice came out lower than I meant it to. Clearing my throat, I added, "What are the top ten movies I should start with?"

"Well now, that's a loaded question. But if I had to pick, I would recommend you start with..." Clove rattled off a list of movies, from action to comedy and everything in between.

I enjoyed listening to her voice as I finished hollowing out my pumpkin and began carving the design I had drawn on it. I glanced up occasionally to see Clove doing the same, completely engrossed in her work and the descriptions she was giving me of her favorite movies. I made a mental note of the ones that sounded especially interesting.

Maybe we could watch some of them together as a way to relax after a long day working in the shop.

I was startled from my thoughts when Silas jumped onto the table from his cat tree, where he'd been watching us through half-lidded eyes. He wove between our pumpkins until he came to a stop in front of the pile of pulp from our pumpkins, which was resting on some newspaper in the middle of the table.

To my surprise, the feline began licking up some of the pulp.

"Um…" I trailed off, raising one eyebrow. "Is it ok for your familiar to be eating that?"

Clove looked up, saw what Silas was doing, and laughed. "Pumpkin is one of his favorite treats. I'm actually surprised it took him this long to take a bite."

"I see." I eyed the cat warily. Silas stared at me with slitted pupils, as if he were accusing me of being a snitch. I was suddenly, uncomfortably aware that my face was well within biting and clawing distance.

It would be nice if I could hear what he was saying.

"No, don't do that Silas," Clove chided him, and I had a feeling I had guessed correctly.

Slowly, I grabbed a piece of the pumpkin shell I had carved out of my design, and held it out to him. "Here, would you like this too?"

Silas leaned forward to sniff the offering, then licked his mouth before darting forward and grabbing the piece of pumpkin out of my hand. I let out a silent breath of relief that his needle-sharp fangs had sunk only into the pumpkin, and not into my hand.

But at least he wasn't glaring at me anymore.

"Silas says thank you," Clove said, but by the way the cat hissed at her, I was guessing her translation was a little off the mark.

Maybe it was a good thing I couldn't hear him telepathically, after all.

"Have you finished carving your pumpkin?" I asked.

She grinned. "Yep! Let's turn them around on the count of three."

"One..." Clove snapped her fingers and little tea candles flew into both of our pumpkins.

"Two..." I grabbed my pumpkin, ready to turn it around.

"Three!"

We both turned our pumpkins to face the other, and my lips curved in a smile when I saw hers. She had carved a cat reaching for the moon.

"Silas, I think that's you." I watched, amused, as the cat puffed out his chest proudly and sat a little straighter, like the cat in the design. I was starting to get an idea of how he was feeling based on his poses, now.

"You have a good eye, Thorne." Clove lit up with delight when her eyes fell on my pumpkin. "Is that a witch hat?"

"I thought it was only appropriate, considering the owner of the shop." My carving wasn't the smoothest, but I was glad she was able to tell at a glance what it was.

"I love it."

"I'm glad." Why did my heart skip a beat when I heard those first two words?

"And...I'm looking forward to attending the Masquerade Ball with you." She looked down shyly, a loose lock of hair falling prettily over her face.

How that foolish warlock had ever looked at another woman when he had this one was beyond me.

"I am, too." A few months ago, the thought of attending an event with that many strangers would have made me want to bolt. In fact, I had been dreading attending it since the moment I agreed to do so. But if it was with her...

Then it no longer sounded so bad.

CHAPTER TWELVE

Secrets & Scones

CLOVE

"**T**oday, I think I'll try your Black Cat Brew," Kana said with a grin. She'd been coming every morning this week since we first opened, and insisted on trying something new every time.

A fox with good taste, Silas commented. *How refreshing.*

"Coming right up." With a flick of my wrist, I had the coffee brewing itself. "I designed this one to boost agility, balance, and the ability to land on your feet—both literally and metaphorically."

"That sounds like exactly what I need right now." Kana propped her hands on her hips and let out a sigh.

"Have there been problems at the bakery?" I asked as I handed Kana her change and her drink.

"Not exactly." Her tails flicked agitatedly. "There's just this...guy who has been visiting nearly every day this week."

"Oh?" I raised an eyebrow. "Has he taken note of your bakery's fabulous *scones?* Or perhaps the fabulous *owner?*"

Kana's cheeks reddened, and she looked a tad flustered. "I'm starting to suspect it's the latter."

"Is he cute?" Then I gave myself a mental kick. Looks only got you so far, as I found out with Rasmus. "Scratch that—is he considerate and respectful?"

"So far? Yes—to both."

"That's a good start, then." I saw the shadows shiver from the corner of my eye, and smiled when Thorne emerged from the back room and joined me. "If you want, Kana, you could invite this guy here for a coffee date sometime—Thorne and I can keep an eye on him."

Kana brightened. "Would you? That would make me feel better."

"You bet." I could practically feel Thorne frowning next to me, but he waited until Kana had left with her coffee to speak.

"I'm not a mercenary for hire anymore," he said quietly.

My eyes widened. "I'm sorry—I didn't mean it like that! I should have asked you first. I just..."

"Just what?" His tone lightened a fraction.

"I feel so safe whenever you're around. I just thought that knowing you were here would help Kana feel at ease, too." I bit my lip.

Thorne's expression softened. He braced his arms on either side of me and leaned in close to murmur in my ear, "You feel safe with me?"

I turned my head slightly, so our faces were only inches apart. "Yes."

The only reason I had not worried at all when Rasmus showed up was because Thorne had been there. Even if our relationship was only for show, I had known that Thorne wouldn't let anyone hurt me.

Of course, I had plenty of defensive spells of my own, not to mention a robust offensive arsenal, but... There was just something about having someone in my corner that freed me to speak my mind without holding back.

I tilted my chin up, and Thorne's violet eyes dropped to my lips. I licked them impulsively, and his eyes tracked the motion. Then he was kissing me, as softly as the rain. He tasted like cinnamon—a spice I had never been overly fond of.

Until him.

"Ahem. Should I come back later?" A teasing voice brought my attention back to the shop—and the customer who had snuck up to the counter like a ninja.

Blushing furiously, I quickly said, "Not at all, Mei. What can I get for you?"

"I'll take a Witchfire Espresso and one of those delicious-looking scones. I think I'm going to need the magical energy boost to get through planning the logistics for this year's Moonlit Masquerade Ball. We're catering it this year."

"I nearly forgot about that!" I'd been so busy preparing to open my own coffee shop that the ball had completely slipped my mind.

"You've had a lot on your plate lately, so I don't blame you." Mei chuckled. "The ball will be in about a week—on Halloween night, of course."

I frowned. "Won't there be a full moon on Halloween this year? Will the werewolves be alright?"

"Yes—your parents will be providing a special brew that will help them stay in their half-shifted forms. That way, the call of the moon won't be as strong, and they can still enjoy the ball on two legs. So long as we make sure they all actually *drink* that potion, of course." Mei rolled her eyes.

"That's good to hear." My smile was tinged with a hint of concern. Mei's golden eyes had dark circles under them. "Is there anything I can do to help?"

Mei brightened. "Actually, if it wouldn't be too much trouble.... Could I ask you to cater the drinks?"

I clapped my hands together. "I'd be delighted!"

"Thank you so much, Clove. That is such a huge weight off my shoulders!" Mei took a long swig of the brew I handed her with a grateful smile. "Now I can just focus on the food. And I'll bring over the funds we reserved for the drinks later tonight."

"That would be great." It might help strengthen my revenue numbers for the month a good deal.

As Mei turned to leave, she winked and called over her shoulder, "And I can't wait to see your matching couple costumes at the ball!"

I blinked, then slowly turned to look at Thorne. We stared at each other for an awkward moment before we both started laughing.

"*Matching* outfits?" The corners of Thorne's mouth twitched up in a smile, despite his best efforts.

"Apparently," I said with a nervous giggle, before clearing my throat. "Though I think we're going about this in the wrong order. I know you've technically already agreed...but let's do this properly." I dropped into a dramatic curtsy. "Sir Thorne, would you do me the honor of accompanying me to the Moonlit Masquerade as my partner?"

Thorne played along, surprising me when he took my hand and bowed, brushing a light kiss on my knuckles. "The honor is all mine, fair lady."

I felt my ears grow warm. "Then it's a date."

"I think I might have some shopping to do, then. And it sounds like we'll both be needing masks," Thorne commented.

"It does indeed." I pursed my lips. "I think the boutique down the street should have what we need, though we should pay them a visit before they're sold out."

"Shall we close up a little early today to go and take a look?" Thorne suggested.

"People rarely come in during the last hour...so let's do it!" It *was* my shop, and I could close early if I wanted to. I loved having that freedom. I grinned, already picturing ballgowns sprinkled with stardust and decorated with pearls.

The end of the day couldn't come soon enough. When it finally did, Thorne and I closed up shop especially quickly–thanks in part to the shadowy figure Thorne summoned to help clean up. Watching it wipe down the tables and sweep the floor made it hard to imagine the peaceful shadow wielding a weapon and fighting monsters.

The owner of Bubbles & Bobbins, the dress boutique, was surprisingly around my age, and from the lyrical sound of her voice, must have been a mermaid.

Her entire boutique was filled with gorgeous dresses and suits, and I caught a glimpse of the line-up of outfits in the back awaiting alterations—no doubt for the upcoming ball.

"It's a good thing you came today—I'll be closed to the public starting tomorrow and until the ball, so that I have enough time to fill all of my orders." Coralyn guided us to a special section with paired mannequins. One pair displayed a fiery red fabric that moved like living flame, and another showed off silk that swayed like it was underwater, with pearls stitched into the bodice and with seashell buttons on the suit.

But it was the pair in the center that really caught my attention. The dress was made of a black, gauzy fabric with purple embellishments and a sprinkling of stardust. The matching suit had turquoise trim and crystal cufflinks that winked like stars in the night sky. As I looked at them, it felt like I was stargazing instead of standing in a boutique.

"We'll take this pair." Thorne gestured to the ones I could hardly take my eyes off of. "Plus the matching masks."

I glanced over at him, glad we were on the same page. I couldn't wait to see how regal he looked in the suit.

"Excellent choice—I have a feeling you will both look splendid in black—and I daresay the violet and turquoise match your eyes perfectly." With a wink, Coralyn moved the two we had picked to the back, with the others. "Now, let me just take your measurements, and I'll make sure they fit like a glove in time for the ball."

"Now, what drinks should we make for the ball?" I mused, tapping my chin thoughtfully. Since we had ordered our outfits yesterday, I could turn my full focus onto catering. "Should I bring some of my more popular drinks, or create something new and special, just for the ball?"

Do you even have enough time to make something new? Silas jumped onto the counter next to me, and I stroked his soft fur.

If it's not too complex. Silas had a point, though. I would hate to bring a half-baked idea that tasted terrible. *Any suggestions?*

How about both? Brew some of your best sellers for the ball, while working on something new. If it doesn't turn out the way you want it, then you'll still have plenty of drinks you know people will love. Silas puffed out his chest and gave his fur a few licks.

That is a fabulous idea!

You say that like all *of my ideas aren't fabulous.* The black cat licked a paw so he could groom his ears.

Good point. Naturally, I would have to bring my pumpkin spice lattes—what drink could be more fitting than that on Halloween?! And a ball in a magical town called for a magical brew, so...I should also bring my Glimmerbrew and Black Cat Brew.

"What are you still doing here? I thought you went home after closing." Thorne detached himself from the shadows.

I had been so deep in thought that I hadn't even noticed the shadows dance at his arrival. "I'm just working out what to make for the ball."

He must have just come out of the shower, because his dark hair was still damp, and his shirt clung to his chiseled form like it was trying to win a wet T-shirt contest.

"Would you like any help?" he asked as he came to stand beside me.

She already has me, Dark One. Silas hissed at him. *And that's more than enough.*

I laughed, and Thorne looked between me and my familiar. "I have a feeling I'm missing something here."

"I would appreciate *both* of your help," I said to mollify them.

No, he reeks. The Dark One can leave. Silas hissed and swatted at Thorne when he tried to come closer. *I've tolerated his presence long enough already.*

Thorne hopped back, with an amused expression on his face. But instead of trying to approach again, he turned around and moved over to the small fridge.

That's right, flee before my magnanimous self. Silas curled his tail around his paws proudly.

"Sorry about him, Thorne. I'm sure he'll come around eventually." Silas usually just left if Thorne got too close, but he was being extra stubborn today for some reason.

"Maybe I can make *eventually* come a little sooner." When he turned around, Thorne was holding a small cup overflowing with whipped cream. The shadowmancer carefully placed it in front of Silas. "A peace offering, from one protector to another."

I hid my smile as I watched Silas' slitted eyes dilate. He sniffed at the mound of fluffy white cream and huffed. *I suppose I will tolerate his presence for today.* Then he began licking up the cream, and proceeded to totally ignore us.

"Is it safe to approach?" Thorne stage-whispered to me.

I hid my smile behind my hand. "It is. You've won him over for tonight—an admirable feat."

"Phew. That's a relief." Thorne gave me a wink as he cautiously came within cat-claw distance.

"Now we can get down to business." I nodded, and brought out some of the more interesting ingredients I'd been saving.

"What are all these?" Thorne asked, peering curiously at them.

"Potential ingredients. I've got some stardust, aurora in a bottle, mermaid's tears, ice from the Northwind's breath, smoked sage, and some mist from an ancient moor." When prepared right, they not only tasted great, but would also have magical effects.

"What would you make with the ice?" Thorne fingered the cork of the bottle.

"A medium roast iced coffee that brings clarity and emotional calm, and can cool even the hottest tempers," I answered. "I'd call it the Frostfang Brew."

"Not bad, though it strikes me more as a summertime drink." He set the vial down gently.

"Good point. I considered maybe the smoked sage or the mist, but those might be too dreary for a festive ball." I drummed my fingernails on the counter.

"How would you use the stardust?"

"In the past, I made a Starfall Cappuccino with it. It enhanced my intuition, made my hair glitter, and gave me visions of possible futures." It had been quite the experience.

Thorne grimaced. "Maybe *not* the best idea to have a room full of magical creatures hallucinating."

I laughed. "You're right, let's save that disaster for another time. That just leaves..." I snapped my fingers, startling Silas, who grumbled at me. "How about an Aurora Affogato?"

"An avocado?" Thorne scrunched up his nose in confusion.

"No, no—an affogato. It's a dessert made by pouring hot coffee over a scoop of ice cream. And if I add in some of my captured aurora..." I flipped open my grimoire to the entry I needed, wanting to double check. "It should cause the drinker to glitter and gleam, and may cause bursts of joy and spontaneous dancing!"

"Bingo! I think you've found the perfect dessert drink for the ball." He smiled at me in a way that set butterflies loose in my stomach. "I think it'll be a big hit with everyone."

"Thanks for brainstorming with me." Rasmus had always written my ideas off, so it was nice to not only be taken seriously, but to have someone willing to help in the developmental stage, and not just as a taste-tester after all the hard work was already done.

I still enjoyed the entire process, though, even if I was doing it alone.

"Who are you thinking about when you get that sad look on your face?" Thorne took a step closer, and gripped my chin gently with his calloused fingers, to force my eyes to meet his.

"No one. I just—how long?" I blurted out. "How long do you plan to stay in Willowmere?"

"I'm...not sure yet," he said, an unreadable expression on his face. "Can I tell you a secret?"

"Anything," I breathed.

"Ever since I ran away from home, I haven't stayed in one place for long. I was afraid to be tied down by relationships with others, only to be uprooted and chased out all over again." Instead of sorrow, his eyes were filled with a sort of wonder. "But that fear...it's starting to fade."

Did he mean that it was fading...because of me?

"Can I tell you a secret?" I repeated, my heart fluttering like a hummingbird's wings.

"Anything," he murmured.

"When I came back home, I swore to myself I would never open myself up to the kind of pain Rasmus put me through again." A lump rose in my throat, but I swallowed it down. "But..."

"But?" he prompted quietly.

"But then you came along." Being this honest scared me. These feelings scared me, especially so soon after my breakup.

Were we moving too fast?

Was I simply fooling myself?

"And you barged right into my bathroom like a wild little thing." He chuckled, and I felt my face flush at the memory. "Then had the *audacity* to put the most feared shadowmancer in the land to work as a barista, of all things."

"And I've appreciated every moment since. Every early morning and every late night." Despite myself, I reached out a hand to trace the thin scar that cut through his eyebrow with my thumb.

If I asked him to stay, would he?

Why was I so afraid to find out?

"I'm happy to help you every day of the week, Clove Morelli." Our faces were inches apart now.

My eyes dropped to his lips, and I found myself wondering what they would taste like covered in stardust and sugar. Thorne closed the gap, pressing his lips against mine with a tenderness that made me ache.

I wrapped my arms around his neck and tangled my fingers in his dark-as-night hair, enjoying the feel of each silky strand. He cupped the back of my head, his other hand going around my waist and tugging me against him. A third, cool caress startled me into opening my eyes to see a tendril of shadow was brushing my hair back from my face.

I laughed against his lips and took his face in my hands. His trim goatee scraped against my hands, which he then kissed, his molten amethyst eyes rooting me to the spot with their intensity.

Thorne kissed me again, so thoroughly that I forgot the names of the stars in the sky.

I could hardly remember the last time I'd felt this at peace, this happy. And that scared me. It made me wonder if something terrible was about to happen, like it always seemed to whenever things went too right in my life.

Was this wise?

Or was I setting myself up to be left behind with another broken heart?

CHAPTER THIRTEEN

Ballgowns & Blows

THORNE

I couldn't stop thinking about the question Clove asked me a couple days ago. The problem was, I didn't really have an answer for her.

When I had wandered into Willowmere, I hadn't exactly had much of a plan. No goal, either. I had simply been surviving with the funds I had amassed from my fighting days, and seeing how long the locals would tolerate my presence.

If I were being honest, I hadn't expected I'd be in Willowmere for this long. Usually, a few months was the best I could hope for.

But then a few months had turned into half a year, and then nearly a full year... And now here I was, pretending to be a witch's boyfriend in exchange for another three months in this peaceful little town. I had never allowed myself to even consider staying here permanently. Staying *anywhere* permanently.

Was that really an option for me?

I had kept my shadow soldiers out of sight up until now. But if I was going to stay, someone else would end up seeing one eventually. I had even started to consider having them help Clove run her shop, for crying out loud!

If I did, would the other residents fear me? Report me to the guild? Try to drag me into some new conflict?

Would I only wind up putting Clove in danger?

Maybe it would be better if I moved on from this town once my three months were up. But by then, would I still have enough conviction left to actually leave?

I doubted it.

It might be better for everyone if I left after the Masquerade Ball. After all, the offer I had received last night from one of the most prestigious guilds in California was rather tempting. Maybe I could stay in Willowmere just long enough to make sure that Rasmus and his mistress left Clove alone.

Even if the mere thought of never seeing Clove again felt like daggers scraping at my heart.

"Here are your fully tailored outfits for the ball, plus their matching masks." Coralyn's lyrical voice broke into my thoughts.

The seamstress held out two large boxes that had been neatly wrapped with a bow. There were dark circles under her ocean-colored eyes, and her normally voluminous hair looked rather deflated.

"Thank you, Coralyn." I took the boxes from her carefully. "Clove and I both really appreciate you fitting us in before the ball—I know you must be terribly busy."

Despite her apparent fatigue, Coralyn's smile was dazzling. "Not at all, darling. I'm always happy to help out gorgeous couples like yourselves." She gave me a wink.

"Your designs do all the heavy lifting. Please accept this as a token of our gratitude." I handed her a few folded bills as a tip.

"Ah, my favorite form of gratitude." She tucked them away into a hidden pocket in her dress. "I just might have to treat myself to a spa day after the ball!"

"You certainly deserve it," I commented as I glanced into the back of her shop, where a line of dresses and suits were still awaiting their alterations.

"Thanks. Say hello to Clove for me!" Coralyn gave me a little wave before she turned and headed towards the back of her boutique and the many gowns she still had to complete.

The mermaid could use an employee or two during the holidays. I supposed if the coffee shop was ever in trouble financially, I could lend out my soldiers as seasonal workers. I huffed a laugh at the thought. From wielding short swords and battleaxes to needles and thread.

My, how my army had fallen.

Or risen, depending on how I looked at it.

Turning, I exited Bubbles & Bobbins and strolled along main street towards The Broom & Bean. My gaze constantly roved for threats; having both of my hands occupied made me uneasy, since it would make defending myself from attacks harder.

But the people strolling along the street in the warm, mid-afternoon light didn't so much as glance in my direction. With the boxes in my hands, I probably looked about as threatening as an errand-boy. The anonymity was...refreshing.

The warlock approaches you from behind, warned one of my shadow soldiers.

Well, it was nice while it lasted.

Though I gave no outward sign of it, I went on high-alert. I subtly shifted most of the packages' weight to my left hand, so my right would be free to wield a shadowsword if needed. Since the sun was high in the sky, I had plenty of shadows to work with.

Now that I was listening for it, I did indeed hear the sound of footsteps behind me. Just one set, so the Maeve Coven witch must not be with him.

When Rasmus reached out to place a hand on my shoulder, I turned sideways to stare at him, leaving his hand hovering in mid-air. The warlock's face froze in surprise for a moment before he plastered a smile on his face. It did not reach his eyes.

"Tom, what a surprise running into you here." He crossed his arms over his chest.

"It's Thorne." I resisted the urge to roll my eyes at his obvious ploy to get a rise out of me. How childish. "And you don't look all that surprised to see me."

"Look, I'm only trying to be polite." Rasmus waved his hands in a gesture of openness, which was when I noticed he was holding a violet rose. A rose the exact same shade as Clove's favorite dress.

"Is that a gift for your...girlfriend, Nora?" I asked pointedly.

His eyebrow twitched when I got his mistress' name wrong. Two could play at that game.

"No, it's not for *Nyssa,*" he ground out through gritted teeth. "It's for my lovely little Clover."

I sharpened my gaze, tempted to rip the rose right out of his hand and crush it. When I didn't say anything, Rasmus began to fidget. Sure enough, he soon cracked under the silent pressure.

"If you *must* know, I intend to ask her to be my partner for the Moonlit Masquerade Ball." His eyes flicked down to the boxes in my hand. "I see she's already sent you to collect her dress, but that won't be necessary; I've already picked out a much more refined one for her that will match my tuxedo."

"I'm afraid you're a little late. Clove will be attending the ball as *my* partner." I stepped closer, using my height advantage to tower over him, while letting wisps of shadow dance in the air between us tauntingly. "So I suggest you magic yourself up a new rose—perhaps a green one, to match the only partner you have left—your *mistress.*"

Beads of sweat formed on his wide forehead. His eyes darting down to the boxes I still held was all the warning I needed.

When magic sparked at his fingertips and his rose transformed into a writhing whip with thorns, I was ready. I dodged to one side and lifted the boxes out of the way before the extending thorns could pierce them and ruin our outfits. My cheek stung, and I felt a trickle of warmth drip down my skin.

All this lazing about had made me rusty.

"How pathetic," I spat. "Even if you *did* destroy her dress, you are the last person Clove would ever attend the ball with!"

I lashed out with my shadows, but scowled when they hit an invisible forcefield and slid harmlessly to the side.

"Nice try," Rasmus said with a smirk. "But you won't be able to get me with the same sneak-attack as last time. And Clove is *mine*—I just need to remind her of that fact, and we can go back to the way things were!"

Summon us, my lord! cried several of my shadow soldiers.

Your lord is not so weak that he cannot handle a single warlock alone, I retorted. *Sit back and watch the show.*

"Clove is her own person—she doesn't belong to anyone," I growled, preparing my shadows. "You chose Nora, and Clove chose me—accept it!"

While Rasmus was sputtering out his reply, I used my shadows to lift the boxes away behind me, and formed a sword made of living shadow in my hand. Before the warlock could process the sight of my new weapon, I had cut through his flimsy barrier and rested the blade at his throat.

He froze, his eyes going impossibly wide. "S-shadows can't cut—"

I increased the pressure just enough to break the skin. The writhing whip in his hand wilted, the spikes shrinking back down into regular-sized thorns.

"Leave Clove alone." My voice took on the rough edge I had used in battle. "If you dare to so much as look at her between now and the ball, your outfit will be the least of your worries."

Rasmus' throat bobbed, and when he realized I was being serious, he slowly nodded. "Fine. Let go already, you stupid adventurer."

My eyes narrowed. His comment reminded me of how he had called me a murderer in front of Clove. My grip tightened, causing the warlock's eyes to widen in fear.

"Would a 'party murderer' let you go?" I hardly recognized my own voice. The anger and resentment I'd been repressing bubbled up to the surface.

"No." Rasmus started shaking, and tears welled in his eyes.

The sight brought me abruptly back to myself. What was I doing? Taking my anger out on this soft warlock wasn't what I should be doing right now.

I had come here for a fresh start, and yet here I was, dwelling in the past and behaving like the sort of adventurer I had so wrongly been accused of being. But unlike before, I had someone waiting for me. Someone for whom I wanted to be a better person.

Without another word, I released Rasmus, who stumbled backwards, but managed to regain his balance before he fell onto the pavement. My shadows returned the boxes to me.

"Move on with your life, Rasmus," I said as I turned to leave. "Clove already has."

Instead of waiting for a reply, I strode away, leaving him staring after me.

Shall I continue to monitor the warlock, my lord? asked the soldier in Rasmus' shadow.

Yes. He's a stubborn mule, so I want him watched until he leaves Willowmere entirely, I replied.

Understood. I will continue my regular reports.

I used the short walk back to The Broom & Bean to get my emotions under control. I took a few deep breaths of the crisp October air, and let the chattering of distant voices and the peaceful chiming of some windchimes soothe my frayed edges.

Before I could use my shadows to open the shop's door, it swung open on its own. Or so I thought, until Silas meowed at me. That cup of whipped cream must have been more effective than I'd thought. I was actually rather touched that the feline had accepted me enough to open the door for me.

"Thanks, Silas. I got a treat for you earlier—remind me to give you your dessert later this evening." He meowed again instead of hissing, so I took that as a good sign.

"I'll send you the map tomorrow for where to drop off the drinks!" Mei called over her shoulder to Clove, as she nearly bumped into me. I steadied her with my shadows. "Oh, hi Thorne! I've got to run, but I'll see you both at the ball!"

"I'll look forward to having some more of your dumplings," I replied as she exited the shop. The firedrake gave me a thumbs-up through the window.

Chuckling to myself, I wove carefully between occupied tables until I made it behind the front counter, where Clove was waiting with an expectant look in her turquoise eyes.

"Coralyn finished the alterations for us," I said with a smile as I set the neatly wrapped boxes on the counter.

"I can't wait to see them," she said excitedly, tracing a finger along the bow. She looked back up to say, "Thanks for picking them up—"

When Clove stared at me, frowning, I stilled. "Clove? What is it?"

"How did this happen?" She reached a hand up to my cheek, her thumb tracing the skin just below the mark left by Rasmus' thorns.

"It's nothing. I wasn't paying enough attention and got pricked by a thorn, is all," I explained smoothly. She had enough to worry about, what with catering the drinks for the ball. I didn't want to add today's little incident to that list.

"Don't lie to me, Thorne," Clove said sternly, with a scowl. "I can sense Rasmus' magic from this wound. What happened?!"

I winced. "Rasmus is perfectly fine, I promise. You don't have to worry about him."

"I'm not worried about *him,*" she said heatedly, and took my face in her hands.

I went very, very still.

"Then..." I trailed off, my eyes searching hers.

"I'm worried about *you!*" The intensity in her gaze rooted me to the spot. "I don't want you getting hurt or in trouble with the sheriff for my sake. I couldn't care less about my ex—so long as he's still breathing somewhere far away from me!"

Had I really considered leaving this woman only a few minutes ago? How could I possibly have considered leaving behind the one and only person in this world who was actually worried about *me* getting hurt, instead of my opponent?

If I wandered away from her now, I knew deep in my bones I would regret it for the rest of my life.

I couldn't hide from the truth or keep denying it any longer. I had fallen for Clove. I had fallen for her from the very first day we met. I had simply been too afraid to admit it, even to myself.

I closed my eyes, melting into her touch. "Rasmus spotted me leaving Bubbles & Bobbins, and tried to ruin your dress. He was under the delusion that you would then go to the ball as his partner if he provided a new dress that matched his outfit for you."

"Of course he did," Clove muttered angrily. "But Thorne, you know you're more important to me than some stupid dress, right?"

"I do now." A lump rose in the back of my throat.

"Good." Clove nodded, and I felt magic start to gather in her fingertips, which hadn't moved from my face. "I hope you made him regret this scratch."

"What sort of shadowmancer worth his salt wouldn't?" I scoffed. "I gave him one to match, with a warning."

"Well done." She gave me a wicked grin. "If the look on his face was anything like the one from the other night when he barged in here, then I'm almost sad I missed it."

Her nose scrunched in concentration, and I felt an itching sensation in my cheek, right where the scratch was.

"There. All healed up." She traced her thumb over the fresh skin where the cut had been, before pulling her hands back.

I didn't let her get far, though. I grabbed her healing hands, and this time, it was her turn to go still.

I kissed her forehead softly. "Thank you. For caring."

"Always."

I smiled. "Now I suppose you had better go try on that dress."

CHAPTER FOURTEEN

Arguments & Affections

CLOVE

"Here are all the drinks." I magically floated over the four hot beverage dispensers to Mei, who was just clearing a spot for them at the drink table.

"Thank you so much, Clove! I never would have been able to handle both the food and the drinks in time." She wiped her brow and flashed me a grateful smile. "I appreciate you coming early to deliver them."

"I'm happy to help—though it's been so long since I last visited the castle, I actually ended up getting lost on the way to the banquet hall." The hallways and staircases were prone to moving, making navigating the castle something of a challenge.

The masquerade was being held in the castle that stood in the forest on the edge of Willowmere. It belonged to one of the original founding families, a vampire clan of a more peaceful and scholarly persuasion. They graciously hosted most of the town's formal events in their grand ballroom.

Mei winked at me. "I get lost every year without fail. Quite embarrassing really, especially when you're pushing a cart filled with food."

"You're telling me." At least I could use my magic to carry the drinks for me. "You look beautiful, by the way. I love your dress!"

"Thank you!" Mei beamed, running her hand along her shimmering golden gown. It matched her eyes, and highlighted the gold tones in her red hair, which was put up in a half-bun. "I love your dress as well—is it also from Bubbles & Bobbins?"

"You guessed it! Coralyn's craftsmanship is outstanding." I loved how the fabric swished with every movement. Fortunately, I had found a set of jewelry made of onyx and amethyst that matched it perfectly.

"I go there for all of my dresses." Mei arranged the branded cups I had brought next to the drink containers. "I can finish up here—why don't you join everyone for the start of the ball?"

"If you're sure you'll be alright..." I trailed off uncertainly.

"Absolutely—I'm almost done, anyways. Just have to arrange the pastries Kana made on the platters." Mei gave me a little wave. "Oh, but don't forget to put on your mask before you enter!"

"Thanks for the reminder!" Now that I was a little more familiar with the landmarks, it was easier to backtrack the way I had come.

The vampires had taken exquisite care of the castle. There was not a single spot of dust on the oil paintings that lined the walls, and every suit of armor was polished until they gleamed in the gently flickering witchlights. The rich carpet kept the sound of my heels from echoing too loudly in the stone hallways, and there was not a single mischievous pixie to be seen.

I took the long way around to the main entrance, where a line of masked gentlemen and ladies were waiting patiently to be announced, so they could descend the stairs into the ballroom. Slipping my mask into place, I joined the line, scanning all the while for Thorne. Though the masks were magical and could conceal the wearer's identity, I had a feeling I'd still be able to spot the shadowmancer.

However, as the line inched forward, I didn't see him anywhere. I had told him to go ahead while I finished preparing the drinks and getting ready, and that I would meet him at the ball. Just as I was starting to wonder if he was already inside, I saw my shadow dance.

"You look stunning," his voice purred in my ear as his hand went around my waist.

"Thank you." I turned to take him in. Thorne looked especially dark and brooding in his pitch black suit. His goatee was neatly trimmed, and his dark hair was styled in a way that reminded me of a wave of shadow poised to crash onto shore. "You look quite dashing, yourself."

"How did the delivery go?" he asked as we inched forward.

"Smoothly—for the most part."

He chuckled. "Don't tell me you got lost."

I scoffed, "Of course not." He simply raised one scarred eyebrow. How did he know me so well? "Okay, maybe a little lost."

"I would have come to find you before long."

I put a hand over my heart and tried not to blush too obviously. Thorne must have noticed, however, because his hand tightened around my waist.

Before long, it was our turn.

I whispered our names to the announcer, and his deep voice echoed throughout the ballroom as we emerged at the top of the grand staircase and began our descent. Lifting my ethereal skirts in one hand, I placed the other in Thorne's hand as I scanned the room below.

The grand ballroom shimmered under the glow of floating jack-o'-lanterns, their carved faces smiling mischievously as they drifted lazily above the heads of the attendees. Velvet of the deepest plum and midnight black hugged the walls, while charmed candles hovered near the ceiling, flickering with flames of ghostly blue and soft amber. A hauntingly sweet melody played from a string quartet in the corner, guiding couples across the polished obsidian floor. I saw faeries in gossamer gowns, werewolves in tailored velvet, and vampires with rose-pinned lapels. Even the shadows seemed to dance, swirling with the scents of cinnamon, autumn leaves, and old magic.

At the heart of the room, a carved crystal pumpkin changed colors every few minutes, and marked the place where the refreshments would be summoned later in the evening. Laughter mingled with the rustle of wings and trailing cloaks, and amidst the swirling magic, it felt like anything was possible.

I quickly spotted Kana in the crowd, and whispered to Thorne that I was going to go greet her while he visited with some of his acquaintances, a werewolf and a strong-looking oni demon. Kana looked divine in a silvery gown covered with blue crystals that glimmered like blue foxfire in the low light. A beaded headdress was draped around her fox ears, and a discreet hole in the back of her dress allowed her tails to move freely.

"I'm so glad you came!" Kana squealed, taking my glove-covered hands in hers.

"I wouldn't miss it for the world," I said warmly. "Especially since I know a certain *someone* supplied the cupcakes for tonight's dessert."

Kana winked. "I have a feeling you'll love them. And I *also* have a feeling there will be an excellent beverage to go with them."

"I recommend the Aurora Affogato—you'll be sparkling and glowing in no time." I loved watching her blue eyes grow round with excitement.

"Thanks for the tip!" She looked around, scanning those around us. "But where's—"

"Your stylish dragon friend? Right here, of course!" Mei said with a grin as she joined us.

"Mei-Mei! I was just starting to wonder if some gentledragon had appeared and spirited you away before all the fun!" Kana teased her with a sly grin.

Mei gave a very unladylike snort. "I wish! Do point me in the direction of any handsome dragons you happen to see. This girl is single, and very much ready to mingle!"

Just then, the string quartet switched from playing soft, ambient music to a far livelier tune.

"The dancing is about to start! Shall we go find ourselves some handsome partners?" Kana asked excitedly.

"I think we can help with that," rumbled an unfamiliar voice.

We turned to see Thorne standing nearby with the werewolf and oni he had been chatting with earlier.

"Would you do me the honor of this dance?" The oni held out his hand to Kana. He looked much like a human, except for the twin horns protruding from his hairline and the red markings on his face.

"I would be delighted." She placed her hand delicately in his, and off they went to the dance floor. I suspected I might be seeing them on a date in my shop sometime soon.

"May I have this dance?" The werewolf offered his hand to Mei, who gracefully accepted.

"Shall we join them, Lady Clove?" Thorne bowed slightly before holding out his hand to me.

"We shall, Sir Thorne." I tried not to grin too broadly as I played along, or to blush too deeply when he brushed a kiss to the back of my hand.

The shadowmancer led us out into the center of the dance floor, among all the swishing skirts and sweeping tails. Thorne placed one hand at my waist and intertwined our fingers, and swept me along in time with the music.

We moved together slowly, the world fading around us. My pulse matched the rhythm of the music, of his breath. Shadows curled lazily around my waist, gentle and supportive.

The music wrapped around us like a warm embrace. Candlelight flickered across his cheekbones, catching in his eyes, which glittered as he watched me. My breath hitched as he twirled me, and adjusted his pace perfectly to match mine. The way he was looking at me, like nothing in the world could tear his gaze away, left me feeling almost dizzy.

No one had ever looked at me like that—not even my former fiancé.

The lively song ended, but neither of us moved to leave the dance floor. The next song started up; a slow waltz. I don't remember when my hand drifted to his chest, resting just over the steady beat of his heart, which seemed to beat in time with mine. I didn't realize when his thumb began to move in slow circles on the back of my hand. And I certainly didn't know why looking up at him suddenly felt like falling and flying at the same time.

I had fallen for him. Completely and utterly. Despite my best efforts, despite my fears, despite every time I had reminded myself that this was pretend, that Thorne was only humoring me in exchange for free rent...he had captured my heart with his shadows. And oh, how warm his shadows turned out to be!

But did he feel the same? I had been such a poor judge of character with Rasmus. Was I about to make the exact same mistake? Or could I trust the emotions I could see in his violet eyes, the ones he had never voiced aloud?

"You're being unusually quiet," I murmured, mostly to break the spell of silence that hung over us like a wave about to crash. Would it sweep me away? Should I risk speaking the question that hovered on my lips?

Thorne tilted his head slightly. "So are you."

I smiled. Even though we hadn't known each other all that long, he still knew me surprisingly well. "Something's been on my mind."

He gave me a rare smile. "Care to share? I'm all ears."

"You still haven't told me," I said, a little breathlessly. "How long you plan to stay in Willowmere."

"A guild in California has asked me to join a raid team for a dungeon they've been having trouble clearing." His words were hard, but his eyes seemed almost sad.

"Does that mean you're leaving soon?" I thought he was done with that sort of life. Why did it feel like my heart was cracking all over again?

"I have to give them an answer by noon tomorrow," he said, dodging the question.

My hope soared. He hadn't decided yet—which meant I still had a chance to convince him to stay.

Thorne held me a little closer as the music shifted into its final notes, both of us lost in thought. I leaned my head on his shoulder, my cheek brushing the soft fabric of his lapel, and closed my eyes. I didn't want to imagine opening the shop every day alone. I knew I would miss seeing the shadows dance when he walked into a room, and the way his casual touches warmed me from the inside out.

As the last chord faded, neither of us moved to let go.

I exhaled, eyes still closed, and whispered, "This doesn't feel like we're pretending anymore." Nerves and anticipation set the butterflies aflutter.

Thorne's breath stirred my hair. "It hasn't for a while now."

My eyes snapped open as a little thrill went through me. If I asked him to stay, would he?

"Thorne, I—"

"Look at these two liars, acting like the world revolves around them," sneered the absolute last voice I wanted to hear.

The room went silent as Rasmus staggered over to us. Nyssa trailed behind him, a smug look on her face. They were wearing matching dark green outfits, but it was the drink in Rasmus' hand that really caught my attention.

He was drunk.

I shot a glare at Nyssa, but she just smirked. How had they found out about my arrangement with Thorne? Not that it mattered now. Could I not have *one* nice event to myself without one or both of these two trying to ruin it?!

"I could say the same of you." A few snickers broke out, and both of their faces flushed. "Could you save your emotional outburst for some other time? In case you hadn't noticed, some of us are trying to enjoy ourselves here."

Thorne set a heavy hand on Rasmus' shoulder. "I think you've had a bit too much to drink, friend." He angled himself in front of me protectively, which only seemed to further enrage him.

"I think everyone here should know that you've been lying to them this whole time!" Rasmus continued as if we hadn't spoken, and roughly shook off Thorne's hand. Now I wasn't the only one shooting them glares.

Should I hex him into silence? But then *I* would look like the bad guy, and everyone here would be distrustful of me, thinking I had something to hide. Which was likely why they had decided to air our dirty laundry in the middle of the ball in the first place. I could see his parents trying to shove their way through the crowd, horrified looks on their faces. But they weren't going to make it in time.

"You and that disgusting shadowmancer have only been *pretending* to date to get back at me, to make me jealous!" Rasmus was beginning to slur his words. "And everyone has a right to know that a monstrous mur—"

Thorne stiffened, his shadows coiling around Rasmus' feet, as if readying to strike. But I wasn't about to let Rasmus make this place a living hell for Thorne because of me.

"Haven't you embarrassed yourself enough, Rasmus?" I snapped, cutting him off. "Not only did you cheat on me, your ex-fiancée, with the witch your pedigree-obsessed parents wished you were marrying, in our bed, but you also chased me all the way here, *mistress in tow,* while pretending to be on a work trip."

After looking into it some more, I had learned that Rasmus wasn't here on business for his coven like he'd first claimed. If

Rasmus had simply left me alone, I would have kept my mouth shut. But of course, he hadn't.

A collective gasp went up, and my face burned. I saw Kana and Mei look at me with pitying expressions, and Rasmus' parents froze, horrified. Even Nyssa had the good sense to look embarrassed. But honestly, what had she expected? That I would just roll over and take it? I may have, once, but that wasn't who I wanted to be anymore.

Rasmus' face turned purple, and a vein throbbed in his forehead. "Shut up, Clover! It was just a little fling! A mistake! Just come home with me, and we'll pretend like nothing ever happened!"

Nyssa looked at him like he'd punched her in the gut. "What? A mistake?!"

He strode forward and grabbed my wrist, yanking me roughly towards him. My heart jumped into my throat and magic gathered at my fingertips

Shadowy vines leaped for Rasmus, wrapping around him, gagging him and completely immobilizing him in seconds. A look of thunderous wrath darkened Thorne's expression as he grabbed Rasmus' wrist and squeezed, until the warlock cried out in pain and he had to release me.

The moment he did, I stumbled back. In an instant, Thorne was behind me. He scooped me up into his arms like I weighed nothing, princess style, and declared to Rasmus and the entire ballroom, "You were right about one thing. Clove asked me to pretend to be her boyfriend to get you to leave her alone. But we're not *pretending* any more. So if you ever so much as breathe in my girlfriend's direction again, don't expect to walk away unscathed again."

I was so busy gaping up at Thorne that I barely even noticed how his shadows formed a cage around both Rasmus and Nyssa, trapping and displaying them on the dance floor like exotic birds for everyone to gawk at.

Before anyone could react, Thorne turned on his heel and carried me out of the ballroom and into the cool night air.

Chapter Fifteen

Shadows & Stars

Clove

"Did you mean what you said?" I whispered, terrified but painfully hopeful. I fisted the fabric of his shirt in my hand as he strode through the gardens that surrounded the castle.

"Every word." Thorne's voice rumbled in his chest, and I could feel his heart racing beneath my ear.

The full moon highlighted the planes of his face, and silvered strands of his hair. When his arms tightened around me, I buried my face in his chest. I felt so relieved and excited and giddy all at once that a laugh bubbled up and snuck its way past my lips.

"Are you crying?" Thorne said in alarm, stiffening for a moment before relaxing when he realized I was laughing. "What's so funny?"

"The looks on their faces," I shook my head in disbelief. "When I first asked you to help me put on a show, I never could have imagined that fiasco in the ballroom."

Thorne sighed, then said ruefully, "They'll be talking about that little scene for *months.*"

"More like years," I corrected him. When he raised a scarred eyebrow at me, I explained, "Magically enhanced lifespans, remember?"

The shadowmancer groaned. "Great. Well, I think we both got a little more than we bargained for out of our little arrangement."

The way his eyes softened when he said that made me think he was referring to more than just the scene we had made. "I'm okay with that."

"Just okay?" His voice went low and husky.

"More than okay." I pressed a lingering kiss to his cheek, and heard his quick intake of breath.

"Good," he growled. "Because I'm not offering refunds. You're stuck with me, now."

"I'm not complaining." On the contrary, I felt like rejoicing. I could hardly believe this was real, that Thorne felt the same way

I did. This whole evening felt magical—minus one unfortunate interruption—in a way that even my most impressive spells couldn't replicate. "Thank you for what you did back there. For protecting me."

Thorne smiled down at me. "I'm sure you could have handled him just fine alone. But I didn't think you should have to."

It was nice, knowing without a shadow of a doubt that Thorne was someone I could rely on. Someone who would see my need and supply it, without having to be asked.

"Where are we going?" I whispered, as we left the castle behind and entered the enchanted forest that surrounded it.

Thorne came to an abrupt halt, as if he hadn't even considered that himself. If he hadn't still been holding me, his answer would have made me weak in the knees. "Home."

Although I had spent four years in that cramped little apartment in Seattle, had it ever really felt like home? I had tried so hard to pretend that it was, but now, only the old brick apartment above my cozy little shop came to mind. Only the touch of cool shadows and the scent of warm cinnamon felt like home.

I smiled into his shirt. "Yes. Let's go home."

The walk back to town was peaceful, and shorter than I would have liked. Thorne didn't ask if I wanted to walk, and I didn't ask him to put me down. I liked feeling safe and cared for in his arms, liked the way the stars reflected in his eyes and the way the crisp autumn breeze cooled my too-warm face.

Trees soon gave way to the quaint little buildings of Willowmere, complete with glowing Jack-o-Lanterns on every porch and balcony. It was almost eerie without other people, as if it were a ghost town.

As Thorne carried me down the main street, lights caught my eye. "Look," I said pointing up at the sky. "They're releasing the lanterns back at the castle."

The Halloween lanterns, which were shaped like pumpkins and had drawn-on faces, swirled across the sky. They glowed like newborn stars as they began their journeys into the endless expanse of the heavens. Though we couldn't see it through the trees, I knew the trail of golden lights led back to the castle.

"Is that some sort of tradition?" Thorne paused to watch them.

"Yes—they're released every year at the end of the ball." I smiled to myself. "It's been years since I've seen it, though. The children are the ones who draw the faces, after they're done trick-or-treating."

We stood watching them dance across the sky in silence for a time. Though the air was cold, Thorne was so warm that I hardly even noticed the chill.

When the last of the lights became pinpricks on the horizon, Thorne carried me the rest of the way to the shop's front door.

But when I made as if to stand, so I could unlock the door, Thorne's arms only tightened around me.

"Thank you Thorne, but you can let me down now." Laughter lightened my tone.

"I've got this." A tendril of shadow slipped into the keyhole and I heard the lock click open.

With a mischievous grin, he swept inside and had his shadows lock the door behind us. He didn't even hesitate once as he navigated through the dark shop without bumping into a single chair or table, and continued up the stairs to the apartment. He unlocked that door just as quickly and easily as the first.

With a flick of my wrist, I sent glowing golden balls of light into the corners of the room, giving the apartment a cozy atmosphere. But the warmth they gave off was nothing compared to what was currently melting me from the inside out.

I reached up and brought his face closer to mine. I breathed in his scent of cinnamon like a drowning sailor seeking air. With a tenderness I had feared I would never feel again, I pressed my lips against his.

"There's something I've been wanting to share with you," Thorne murmured.

Shadows erupted around us and formed into a massive cocoon. It was so dark I couldn't see my hand in front of my face, but I wasn't worried for a moment—not when I could feel Thorne's arms around me.

When the darkness faded, we were standing on what must have been the roof of the building. But next to the chimney, I spotted a thick blanket draped across the shingles. Thorne carried me over to it, and knelt to gently place me on top of the blanket before sitting down next to me.

"I like to come up here whenever I need to clear my head," he explained. "Since Willowmere is surrounded by the forest, this is one of the best places to see the stars."

I looked up, and was awed by what I saw. The stars looked like they had been scattered across a bed of crushed velvet. They sparkled as brightly as diamonds and glimmered with their own inner magic. Splashes of deep indigo and violet made the entire view look like one big painting. In the distance, I could even make out some of the glowing paper lanterns from the ball as they drifted along in the breeze.

"You can still see the lanterns from up here," I murmured with a smile. "It makes everything else seem so small."

"It does help put things into perspective," he agreed. "Which is why coming up here always reminds me how small my doubts and fears really are, in the grand scheme of things."

There was a vulnerability in the way he said that, that made my breath hitch. Based on how he kept a blanket up here, I had a feeling that he frequented this refuge more often than he cared to admit.

"On the nights when Rasmus was snoring soundly next to me, completely oblivious to the way I was wondering if I was truly following the right path, I would cast a spell on the ceiling to show me the sky, instead." Only Silas knew about this particular secret of mine. I had kept my doubts hidden, even from my closest friends.

"Did you ever make a wish on a shooting star?"

It felt like he could see right through me. "Every time."

"What would you wish for?"

"A life worth living." I had never given voice to it before.

His violet eyes bored into mine. "Has your wish come true yet?"

"It has—just now, in fact," I admitted softly. "Now I'm near my parents and friends, I have my own business that allows me creative freedom, and…I've found someone to share my life with."

"What a coincidence." His smile was so radiant I nearly had to close my eyes. When we first met, he had hardly ever smiled. But over the last few days, Thorne smiled every time he looked at me—and I could hardly get enough of the sight. "My wish has also come true."

The way he was looking at me made me think that I was the fulfillment of his wish, just as he was the fulfillment of mine.

"Thank you for sharing it with me, Thorne." I laced my fingers through his. "This place is beautiful."

"It's not nearly as beautiful as you."

This felt surreal, like a dream—the kind I never wanted to wake up from. But I was afraid that, when I did, Thorne would be gone. But if we were both being vulnerable tonight, then...

"Sometimes, you make me worry that just like your shadows, you'll disappear in the blink of an eye." I removed his mask so I could see his expression properly, setting it aside.

His breath hitched. "Before I came to Willowmere, it was easy for me to slip away, to move on to the next town. No one else has ever tried to hold onto me like you have." He removed my mask with a tenderness that warmed my heart.

Strands of dark hair fell over his eyes, and I could feel a slight tremor coming from the hand I held. Maybe it was the way he was looking at me, but I felt brave—brave enough to ask the question that had been hovering on my lips for days.

"If I asked you to stay, would you?" I held my breath as I waited for his answer.

"Ask me, and find out." His violet eyes drew me into their depths like a cat drawn to a hearth.

"Will you stay with me?" I murmured, raising one hand to his cheek. "As my real boyfriend, this time?"

"Yes." He leaned into my touch.

I felt so happy I could float.

"You have no idea what it does to me when you look at me like that," he murmured, resting his forehead against mine.

"Like what?"

"Like I'm someone worth loving," he whispered, with a raw pain in his voice that made my heart ache.

"But you are. Always have been, always will be."

"Will you have me, scars, shadows and all?"

"Scars, shadows and all."

Before I had even finished speaking, Thorne's lips were on mine. I tangled my fingers in his silky black hair, and a spark of my magic filled his dark locks with thousands of glittering little stars, that paled in comparison to the ones shining above us.

I had never felt this way before. I had never felt so wholly seen. So wholly protected. So wholly loved.

"I love you." The words were out before I could snatch them back.

"I love you, too." His voice was low, husky. Sparks of violet magic popped in the air around us like miniature fireworks, responding to my jubilant emotions.

He kissed me just as a shooting star streaked across the sky, like a bolt of magic in the darkness. When he draped his arm around my shoulders, I snuggled up against him, even as my heart sighed in contentment and slowed, and my eyelids began to droop.

"Would you like to stay the night?" Thorned murmured, pressing a light kiss to my hair.

"Yes." I shivered in the cool October air, and Thorne hugged me closer. "Will you have me, magic, mochas and all?"

I wanted to hear him say it, too.

"Magic, mochas and all."

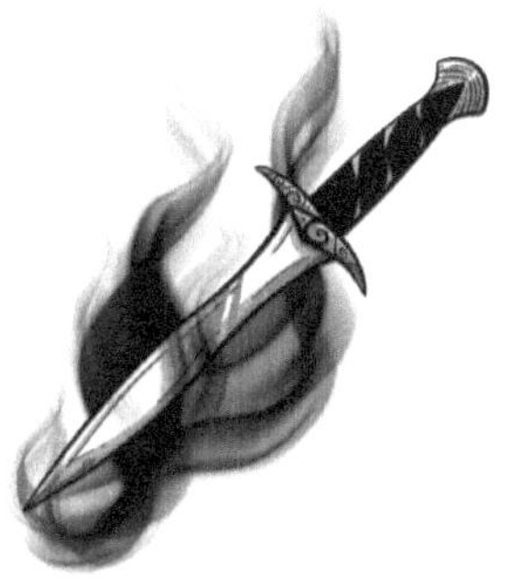

Epilogue

THORNE

The warm sunlight flickering across my face woke me. When I blinked open my eyes, I froze, hardly daring to breathe. Next to me, her face softened in sleep, was Clove.

Last night had been so perfect that I had nearly convinced myself it was just a dream—that when I woke up, I would be alone. Just like always.

But there she was, her chest rising and falling with each breath. Her long, dark hair was splayed over my pillow. Impulsively, I lifted a lock of it, letting the silky strands slip through my calloused fingers.

I lay there watching her for a few minutes, marveling at the beautiful witch who had brought light back to my world of darkness. I couldn't help but smile. For the first time in my life, I found myself imagining what it would be like to build a future for myself. A future with *her*. One filled with the smell of coffee and the sound of easy laughter. With slow, cozy days and magical, starry nights.

An ordinary life, with an extraordinary woman.

I glanced at the clock on my bedside table, grimacing when I saw the time. My extraordinary woman would definitely give me an earful if I didn't wake her up in time to open the shop. But maybe I could let her sleep just a little longer if I got things rolling.

Silently, I summoned one of my shadow soldiers, and commanded it to begin doing her usual opening procedures: Counting the cash in the register, setting up the tables and chairs, turning on the lights, etc. If the locals became accustomed enough to them, then I might even be able to have them work as baristas for her during the day.

I stole a few minutes more in bed, savoring her warmth, and the peaceful expression on her face. She had been so brave last night, standing up to that moron of a warlock and his mistress in front of everybody like that. I was proud of her. But it was a pity she hadn't gotten to see everyone's reactions to her Aurora Avocado—er, Affacato? Affagato? I rolled my eyes at myself. To her ice cream coffee concoction.

At least we would have the chance to see their reactions at the ball next year.

As quietly as I could, I swung my legs out from under the covers and eased out of bed. Despite my near-wraithlike silence, Clove stirred, frowning and mumbling.

"Go back to sleep, love," I murmured, leaning over her and kissing her lightly on the forehead.

Her troubled expression smoothed, and Clove's breathing evened out once more. I smiled to myself.

I donned my robe and padded out of my bedroom and down to the shop. My shadow was doing a good job getting everything ready. I did a double-take when I glanced at the front door, and spotted the kitsune girl—Kana—peering into the window, a box propped against her hip.

I had completely forgotten she always delivered her fresh pastries early. Striding over to the door, I unlocked it and motioned her inside. "Good morning, Kana. How you get up so early every day is a mystery to me."

"Morning, Thorne," she said with a chipperness that made me feel tired. Her blue eyes looked me up and down in an appraising fashion, and she gave me a sly grin. "So, how is Clove doing this morning?"

I blinked. "What makes you think Clove is here, instead of at her parents' place?"

Her foxy grin stretched wider, and she chuckled. "After the way you princess-carried her out of the castle like her dark knight in shadow armor? Please. Give a girl a little credit."

I felt the tips of my ears grow warm, and cleared my throat awkwardly. "Clove is still sleeping."

"Good. She deserves some solid rest." She nodded to herself, not looking at all surprised, and set the box down on the counter. She glanced at my shadow soldier, but didn't seem bothered by it in the least. "I brought over chocolate cupcakes today—her favorite."

Kana gave me a wink.

"Thank you. I was going to make her a mocha in bed, and I might just have to bring her one of your cupcakes," I admitted.

"That is a *marvelous* idea. You can never have too much chocolate, after all." She headed back to the door, and said, "I'll stop by later to spill all the tea to Clove about what happened after you two left—and how big of a hit her dessert was."

And with a little wave and a swish of her tails, she practically skipped out the door and back to her bakery. I chuckled to myself. She was quite the character, that one.

Turning back to the counter, I took her box and pulled out the cupcake that had the most frosting, setting it aside for Clove. I then instructed my soldier to carefully place the rest of the cupcakes in the display case while I set about making her mocha.

I made sure to craft it exactly the way she liked it, and topped it off with a generous amount of whipped cream and a sprinkling of chocolate shavings. After whipping up a little something for me, too, I set everything on a little tray and carried it up the stairs, being extra careful not to spill a single drop.

I lingered for a moment by my bedroom door, just savoring the sight of her. On silent feet, I padded over to the bedside table and placed the tray there.

"Good morning, love," I murmured, pressing a kiss to her forehead. "It's time to wake up."

"Mhmm," she moaned, before rolling over and promptly going back to sleep.

I laughed, then grabbed the cupcake and held it under her nose. Her eyes flew open, and Clove stared at the pastry in bewilderment. "Chocolate?"

I put the cupcake back on the tray, and set it on her lap after she sat up. Clove looked up at me with those big turquoise eyes of hers with an expression that bordered between surprise and happiness.

"You made me breakfast?"

"Well, if you can call a cupcake and a mocha breakfast," I said as I climbed back into bed, my own mocha in hand.

Clove smiled so widely that even her eyes seemed to sparkle. "I call it the breakfast of champions!"

"Glad to hear it. Though I can't take all the credit—Kana brought the cupcakes by earlier," I admitted.

"Wait, what time is it?" Clove froze, her head whipping around until her eyes landed on my clock. "Oh no, is it that late already?! I have to get ready to open the shop!"

I put my hand over hers before she could jump out of bed, and she stilled immediately.

"Clove, relax. I have one of my shadows doing all of the opening procedures right now. Finish your cupcake first, and then you can take your time getting ready. Besides, after last night, I highly doubt anyone will be hauling their butts out of bed until at least ten." I rubbed soothing circles into the velvety-soft skin on the back of her hand.

"Really?" Her eyes went round as she met my gaze. "You did all that for me?"

How little had Rasmus done for her that something so simple impressed her like this?

"Really. And you'd better get used to it, because I'm not going anywhere. After my three months are up, even that sour-faced centaur won't be able to kick me out of here."

Clove leaned over and pecked me on the cheek.

"What was that for?" I asked, my voice taking on a husky edge that had Clove's cheeks turning that adorable shade of pink.

"For staying," she answered simply.

A whole party of adventurers wouldn't be able to tear me away from this place now. I was well and truly smitten.

"Would you like to stay? With me?" I had molded a wisp of shadow into a key. "Though this is technically *your* apartment, after all."

Clove grabbed my face and pressed her lips to mine. "Yes," she breathed, and rested her forehead against mine. The aroma of chocolate perfumed the air between us.

I slid my hand into her hair, and kissed away the rest of the frosting that lingered on her lips. She melted into my touch, and if she had been a cat, I think she would have been purring. Hopefully, her familiar would get used to me eventually. But I was confident I would win him over—no matter how many cups of whipped cream it took.

Suddenly, her eyes lit up. "I just got the best idea for a new drink to add to the menu!"

I chuckled, leaning back. "Oh? And what would that be?"

"I think I'll call it the ShadowSpice Latte." She got that dreamy look in her eyes she always did when she talked about coffee. "Inspired by my very own shadowmancer. Will you help me perfect it?"

"I would love to." I laced my fingers through hers, as she went back to inhaling her cupcake and mocha.

I took a sip of my own mocha and hid my grimace.

I had never liked coffee. The bitter flavor was just not something I enjoyed, even masked with vanilla or chocolate or pumpkin spice. But I had the feeling I would eventually grow to love it, too.

Because the magic I had found with Clove was more than worth putting up with drinking a mocha every day for the rest of my life. In fact, I would be happy to, if it meant staying right here by her side.

Acknowledgements

I wanted to include a special thank you to all of my wonderful backers on Kickstarter! This project truly could not have been brought to life without all of your support.

I would also like to thank Jessica, my cover designer, for her absolutely beautiful work. I couldn't have asked for a better cover. And thanks, as always, to my alpha reader Aly, for all your feedback and encouragement.

Also by Vanna Woods

<u>Tales of Love & Lore</u>

Magic & Mochas

Dragons & Dumplings

Nymphs & Nutcrackers

Foxes & Frosting

About the Author

Vanna Woods is a lifelong lover of magical stories, art of all kinds, and a really good hot chocolate. When she's not writing cozy romances filled with charm and heart, you can find her curled up with a fantasy novel, sketching dreamy characters in one of her many sketchbooks, or gliding across the ice at the local rink.